IN THE LAST ANALYSIS

"A rare pleasure . . . the American intellectual crime novel at its brightest and best."

Francis Iles

"I had a wonderful time with *In the Last Analysis*. There I sat, all alone in the house, and laughed aloud over the felicity of some of the dialogue. It was all delightfully entertaining . . . I do think this is a very good book."

Charlotte Armstrong

"A splendid puzzle of people, with dimension and purpose."

Dorothy Salisbury Davis

"Written with real sparkle and charm . . . Miss Cross carries you along with such ease and good humour."

Julian Symons

AMANDA CROSS

When the ingenious Kate Fansler made her debut in this novel, Anthony Boucher of *The New York Times* called her "an amateur detective in the finest tradition." She would later star in THE THEBAN MYSTERIES, THE QUESTION OF MAX, and POETIC JUSTICE, also available from Avon.

Other Avon Books by
Amanda Cross

POETIC JUSTICE
THE QUESTION OF MAX
THE THEBAN MYSTERIES

AMANDA CROSS

IN THE LAST ANALYSIS

AVON
PUBLISHERS OF BARD, CAMELOT, DISCUS AND FLARE BOOKS

AVON BOOKS
A division of
The Hearst Corporation
1790 Broadway
New York, New York 10019

Copyright © 1964 by Carolyn Heilbrun
Published by arrangement with the author
Library of Congress Catalog Card Number: 64-11757
ISBN: 0-380-54510-1

First Avon Printing, March, 1966

AVON TRADEMARK REG. U.S. PAT. OFF. AND IN
OTHER COUNTRIES, MARCA REGISTRADA,
HECHO EN U.S.A.

Printed in the U.S.A.
WFH 10 9 8 7

prologue

"I DIDN'T say I objected to Freud," Kate said. "I said I objected to what Joyce called freudful errors—all those nonsensical conclusions leaped to by people with no reticence and less mind."

"If you are going to hold psychiatry responsible for sadistic parlor games, I see no point in continuing the discussion," Emanuel answered. But they would continue the discussion nonetheless; it had gone on for years, and showed no signs of exhausting itself.

"By the way," Kate said, "I've sent you a patient. At any rate, a student asked me to recommend a psychoanalyst, and I gave her your name and address. I have no idea if she'll call, but I rather expect she will. Her name is Janet Harrison." Kate walked to the window and looked out on the raw and blustery weather. It was the sort of January day when even she, who loathed spring, longed for it.

"Considering your opinion of psychiatry," Nicola said, "Emanuel should feel duly honored. Look honored, Emanuel!" Nicola, Emanuel's wife, followed these discussions rather as the spectator at a tennis match follows the ball, her head turning from one to the other. Having managed to place her faith in psychiatry without withdrawing her right to criticize, she applauded the good shots and groaned at the misses. Kate and Emanuel, charmed with Nicola as audience, enjoyed the matches not only for the occasional insights which emerged from them, but also because they shared the knack of irritating without ever offending each other. Nicola smiled on them both.

"It isn't Freud himself one quarrels with," Kate said, "nor even the great body of theory he evolved. It's the dissemination of his ideas in the modern world. I'm always reminded of the story of the Japanese gentleman and the

Trinity: 'Honorable Father, very good; Honorable Son, very good; but Honorable Bird I do not understand at all.' "

"Your quotations," Emanuel said, "always enliven the conversation without in any way advancing the discussion."

"The only quotation I can think of," said Nicola, in her turn walking to the window, "is 'If Winter comes, can Spring be far behind?' "

Which, as it turned out, was the most significant remark anybody made that afternoon.

chapter 1

SOMEONE had chalked "April is the cruelest month" on the steps of Baldwin Hall. Kate, unimpressed by the erudition, agreed with the sentiment. Spring on an American campus, even as urban a campus as this one, inevitably drove the faculty into a mood compounded of lassitude, irritation and fastidiousness. Perhaps, Kate thought, it is because we are getting old, while the students, like Caesar's crowds on the Appian Way, are always the same age. Gazing at the students who sprawled, or made love, on every available patch of grass, Kate longed, as she did each spring, for a statelier, less untidy era. "The young in one another's arms," Yeats had complained.

She mentioned this to Professor Anderson, who had stopped too, pondering the chalk inscription. "This time of year," he said, "I always want to shut myself up in a dark room, with the curtains drawn, and play Bach. Really, you know," he said, still regarding Eliot's line, "Millay put it better: 'To what purpose, April, do you return again?'" Kate was startled by Professor Anderson, who was an eighteenth century man with a strong distaste for all female writers since Jane Austen. Together they entered the building and mounted the stairs to the English department on the next floor. That was it, really. However expected, April was always startling.

On the bench outside Kate's office, waiting for her office hours, sat a line of students. This too was a spring symptom. The good students either vanished from the campus altogether, or appeared at odd moments to argue some abstruse point of interpretation. The mediocre, particularly the poor ones, began to worry about marks. April, stirring their dull senses, reminded them that the time of marks was near and the B they had faithfully promised themselves dismally remote. They had come to talk it out. Kate sighed as she unlocked the door to her office, and then stopped, in surprise and annoyance. A man standing at the window turned as she entered.

"Please come in, Miss Fansler. Perhaps I should say Doctor, or Professor; I am Acting Captain Stern, Detective from the Police Department. I've shown my credentials to the secretary in the office, who suggested that I had perhaps better wait in here. She was kind enough to let me in. I haven't disturbed anything. Won't you sit down?"

"I assure you, Captain," Kate said, sitting down at her desk, "I know very little about the personal lives of my students. Has one of them got into trouble?" She regarded the detective with interest. An avid reader of detective stories, she had always suspected that in real life detectives were desperately ordinary men, the sort who coped well with short-answer exams (corrected by machine) but were annoyed by complex ideas, literary or otherwise; the sort who liked the hardness of facts and found the need for ambivalence distasteful.

"Would you be good enough to tell me, Miss Fansler, what you were doing yesterday morning until noon?"

"What I was *doing?* Really, Captain Stern, I do assure you that . . ."

"If you will just be good enough to answer my questions, Miss Fansler, I will explain the reasons for them very shortly. Yesterday morning?"

Kate stared at him, and then shrugged. As is the unfortunate habit of the literary person, she already imagined herself retelling this extraordinary event. She caught the detective's eye, and reached for a cigarette. He lit it for her, waiting patiently. "I don't teach on Tuesdays," she said. "I am writing a book, and I spent all yesterday morning in the stacks of the library, looking up articles in nineteenth century periodicals. I was there until a little before one, when I went to wash, and then to meet Professor Popper for lunch. We ate in the faculty club."

"Do you live alone, Miss Fansler?"

"Yes."

"What time did you arrive in the 'stacks'?"

"The stacks, Captain Stern, are the inner floors of the

library, on which the books are kept." Why is it, she wondered, that women are always annoyed at being asked if they live alone? "I got to the library at about nine-thirty."

"Did anyone see you in the stacks?"

"Anyone who could give me an 'alibi'? No. I found the volumes I wanted, and worked with them at the small tables along the wall provided for that purpose. Several people must have seen me there, but whether they recognized me, or remembered me, I couldn't say."

"Do you have a student named Janet Harrison?"

In books, Kate thought, detectives were always enthusiastically interested in their work, rather like knights on a quest. It had never really occurred to her before with what fervor they attacked their work. Some of the time, of course, they were related to, or in love with, the accused or murdered, but whether being a detective was their job or avocation, they seemed vehemently to care. She wondered what, if anything, Acting Captain Stern cared about. Could she ask him if he lived alone? Certainly not. "Janet Harrison? She used to be a student of mine; that is, she took one of my classes, on the nineteenth century novel. That was last semester; I haven't seen her since." Kate thought longingly of Lord Peter Wimsey; at this point, surely, he would have paused to discuss the nineteenth century novel. Captain Stern seemed never to have heard of it.

"Did you recommend that she attend a psychoanalyst?"

"Good God," Kate said, "is that what this has to do with? Surely the police are not checking up on all people who attend analysts. I didn't 'recommend' that she attend an analyst; I would consider it improper to do any such thing. She came to me having already decided, or been advised, to go to an analyst. She asked me if I could recommend a good one, since she had heard of the importance of finding a properly qualified man. Now that you mention it, I don't quite know why she came to me; I suppose we are all too willing to assume that others recognize us as monuments of good sense and natural authorities on most things."

There was no answering smile from Captain Stern. "Did you in fact recommend a psychoanalyst?"

"Yes, in fact, I did!"

"What was the name of the analyst you recommended?"

Kate was suddenly angry. Glancing out of the window, where April was breeding desire all over the place, did nothing to improve her mood. She averted her eyes from the campus and looked at the detective, who appeared unmoved by April. Undoubtedly he found all months equally cruel. Whatever this was about—and her curiosity had been greatly diluted by annoyance—was there any purpose in dragging Emanuel into it? "Captain Stern," she asked, "am I required to answer that question? I'm not at all certain of the legal rights in this matter, but wouldn't I be 'booked,' or told what this is all about, if I'm to answer questions? Would it suffice for now if I were to assure you (though I cannot prove it) that yesterday morning until one o'clock I was involved in no way whatever with any human being other than Thomas Carlyle, whose death well over half a century ago precludes the possibility of my having been in any way involved in it?"

Captain Stern ignored this. "You say you did recommend a psychoanalyst to Janet Harrison. Did she find him satisfactory; did she plan to continue with him for very long?"

"I don't know," Kate said, feeling somewhat ashamed of her outburst into sarcasm, "I don't even know if she went to him. I gave her his name, address and telephone number. I mentioned the matter to him. From that moment to this I haven't seen the girl, nor given her a moment's thought."

"Surely the analyst would have mentioned the matter to you, if he had taken her as a patient. Particularly," Captain Stern added, revealing for the first time a certain store of knowledge, "if he were a good friend."

Kate stared at him. At least, she thought, we are not playing twenty questions. "I can't make you believe it, of course, but he did not mention it, nor would a first-rate analyst do so, particularly if I had not asked him. The man in question is a member of the New York Psychoanalytic Institute, and it is against their principles ever to discuss a patient. This may seem strange; nonetheless, it is the simple truth."

"What sort of girl was Janet Harrison?"

Kate leaned back in the chair, trying to gauge the man's intelligence. She had learned as a college teacher that if

10

one simplified what one wished to say, one falsified it. It was possible only to say what one meant, as clearly as possible. What could this Janet Harrison have done? Were they trying to establish her instability? Really, this laconic policeman was most trying.

"Captain Stern, while the students are attending classes here, their lives are going on; most of these students are not isolated in dormitories, they are not away from family pressure, financial pressures, emotional pressures of all sorts. They are at an age when, if they are not married—and that is a state which brings its own problems—they are suffering from love or the lack of it. They are going to bed with someone they love, which is to be in one emotional state, or they are going to bed with someone they do not love, which is to be in another, or they are going to bed with no one at all, which is to be in still another. Sometimes they are colored, or the unreligious children of religious parents, or the religious children of unreligious parents. Sometimes they are women torn between mind and family. Often they are in trouble, of one sort or another. As teachers, we know little of this, and if we catch a hint of some of it we are—how shall I put it—not the priest, but the church: we are there; we continue. We speak for something that goes on—art, or science, or history. Of course, we get the occasional student who tells you about himself even as he breathes; for the most part, we get only the most general impression, apart, of course, from the student's actual work.

"You ask what sort of girl was Janet Harrison? I tell you all this so that you will understand my answer. I have only an impression. If you ask, Was she the sort to hold up a bank? I would say No, she didn't seem to me the sort, but I'm not sure I could tell you why. She was an intelligent student, well above the average; she gave me the impression of being able to do excellent work, should she put her mind to it, but her whole mind was never put to it. It was as though a part of her was off somewhere, waiting to see what would happen. Yet you know," Kate added, "till you asked me, I had not thought of it quite that way."

"Didn't you have any idea why she would want to go to a psychoanalyst?"

"No, I did not. People today turn to analysis as they

11

used to turn to—what? God, their minister, their families; I don't pretend to know. I have heard people say, and only half in fun, that parents had better save now for their child's analysis as they used to save for his college education. A youngster today, moving in intellectual circles, will, in trouble, turn to psychiatry, and his parents will often help him if they can."

"And a psychiatrist, a psychoanalyst, will accept any patient who comes to him?"

"Of course not," Kate said. "But surely you haven't come here to learn about these matters from me. There are many people competent to discuss . . ."

"You sent this girl to a psychoanalyst, and he took her as a patient. I would like to know why you thought she should go to an analyst, and why you thought this analyst would take her."

"This is my office hour," Kate said. Not that she minded, on this particular April day, missing the students ("I'm a provisional student, Professor Fansler, and if I don't get a B- in this course . . ."), but the thought of the students patiently waiting on the bench, perhaps now overflowing it . . . but Captain Stern had no objection, obviously, to displacing the students. Perhaps she should send Captain Stern to Emanuel. All at once, the thought of sitting in her office on a spring day, discussing psychiatry with a police detective, struck her as ludicrous. "Look here, Captain Stern," she said, "what is it you want to know? Before a good analyst will take on a patient, he must be certain that the patient is qualified for analysis. The patient must be of sufficient intelligence, with certain kinds of problems, with a certain possibility for free development. A psychotic, even certain neurotics, are not proper subjects. Most of all, a patient must *want* to go into analysis, must *want* to be helped. On the other hand, most analysts that I have met believe that any intelligent person can be helped, can be given a greater freedom of activity by a good analysis. If I am asked to recommend a good analyst, I recommend a good one, knowing that a good analyst will only take a patient suitable to analysis, and suitable to analysis by this particular analyst. I can't be any clearer than that on a subject about which I know remarkably little, and any psychiatrist hearing me now would probably scream in horror

12

and say I'd got it all wrong, which I probably have. Now what in the world has Janet Harrison done?"

"She has been murdered."

Captain Stern left the words hanging in the air. From outside came the campus noises of spring. Some fraternity boys were selling raffle tickets on a car. The shadow of someone, probably a student, passed back and forth behind the glass door to Kate's office.

"Murdered?" Kate said. "But I knew nothing about her. Was she attacked in the street?" Suddenly the girl seemed born again in Kate's memory, sitting where Captain Stern now sat. *Thou art a scholar; speak to it, Horatio.*

"You said, Miss Fansler, she seemed to be waiting to see what would happen. What did you mean by that?"

"Did I say that? I don't know what I meant. A way of speaking."

"Was there *anything* of a personal nature between you and Janet Harrison?"

"No. She was a student." Suddenly, Kate remembered his first question: *What were you doing yesterday morning?* "Captain Stern, what has this to do with me? Because I gave her the name of an analyst, because she was my student, am I supposed to know who murdered her?"

Captain Stern rose to his feet. "Forgive me for taking the time from your students, Miss Fansler. If I have to see you again, I will try to make it at a more convenient hour. Thank you for answering my questions." He paused a moment, as though arranging his sentences.

"Janet Harrison was murdered in the office of the psychoanalyst to whom you sent her. Emanuel Bauer is his name. She had been his patient for seven weeks. She was murdered on the couch in his office, the couch on which, as I understand it, patients lie during their analytic hour. She was stabbed with a knife from the Bauer kitchen. We are anxious, of course, to find out all we can about her. There seems to be remarkably little information available. Goodbye for now, Miss Fansler."

Kate stared after him as he left, closing the door behind him. She had underestimated his flair for the dramatic; that much was clear. *I've sent you a patient, Emanuel.* What had she sent him? Where was he now? Surely the police could not imagine that Emanuel had stabbed a patient on his own couch? But how then had the murderer got in? Had Emanuel been there? She picked up the receiver and dialed 9 for an outside line. What was his number? She would not thumb through a phone book. It surprised her to notice, as she dialed 411 for information, that her hand was shaking. "Can you give me the number, please, of Mrs. Nicola Bauer, 879 Fifth Avenue?" Emanuel's office number was under his name, his home phone under Nicola's, she remembered that: to prevent patients calling him at home. "Thank you, operator." She did not write it down, but repeated it over and over to herself. Trafalgar 9. But she had forgotten to dial 9 again for an outside line. Begin again and take it slowly. *Emanuel, what have I done to you?* "Hello." It was Pandora, the Bauers' maid. What an amusing name it had once seemed! "Pandora, this is Miss Fansler, Kate Fansler. Please tell Mrs. Bauer that I must speak to her."

"Just a minute, Miss Fansler, I'll see." The phone was laid down. Kate could hear one of the Bauer boys. Then there was Nicola.

"Kate. I suppose you've heard."

"A detective's been here; I'm in my office. Efficient, laconic, and, I suspect, superficial. Nicki, are they letting you stay there?"

"Oh, yes. Thousands of men have been through the whole place, but they say we can stay. Mother said we should go home with her, but once the policemen cleared out, it seemed better somehow to stay. As though if we left, we might never come back, Emanuel might never come back. We've even kept the boys here. It does seem crazy, I suppose."

"No, Nicki. I understand. You stay. Can I come and see you? Will you tell me what's happened? Will they let me come?"

"They've only left a policeman outside, to cope with the mobs. There've been reporters. We'd like to see you, Kate."

"You sound exhausted, but I'm coming anyway."

"I'd like to see you. I don't know about Emanuel. Kate, I think they think we did it, in Emanuel's office. Kate, don't you know an Assistant District Attorney? Maybe you could . . ."

"Nicki, I'll be right over. I'll do anything I can. I'm leaving now."

Outside the office a few students still waited. Kate rushed past them down the stairs. On that bench, how many months ago, Janet Harrison had waited. *Professor Fansler, could you recommend a good psychiatrist?*

chapter 2

THERE is no real reason why psychiatrists should confine themselves to the most elegant residential section of the city. Broadway, for example, is accessible by subway, while Fifth, Madison, Park Avenue, and the side streets which connect them can be reached only by taxi, bus or on foot. But no psychiatrist would dream of moving west, with the exception of a few brave souls on Central Park West, who apparently find sufficient elegance in the sight of Fifth Avenue across the park. Whether this has formed itself as an equation: East Side = style, psychiatry = style, therefore psychiatry = East Side; whether it is that the West Side and success are unthinkable together, whatever the reason, psychiatrists find themselves, and their patients find them, in the sixties, seventies, perhaps the low eighties, between the avenues. The area is known, in certain circles, as psychiatrists' row.

The Bauers lived in a ground-floor apartment in the sixties, just off Fifth Avenue. The building itself was on Fifth Avenue, but Dr. Emanuel Bauer's office address was 3 East. This added, for some mysterious reason, a note of elegance, as though, living on Fifth Avenue, it was more couth if one did not say so in so many words. What the Bauers' rent was, Kate had never dared to imagine. Nicola, of course, had money, and since Emanuel's office was in the apartment, a percentage of the rent was tax deductible. Kate herself lived in a large four-room apartment overlooking the Hudson River, not, as some of her friends said, because she was a reverse snob, but because the old apartments on the East Side were unavailable, and as for the new ones—Kate would rather have pitched a tent than live with a windowless kitchen, with walls

16

so thin one listened, perforce, to the neighbors' television, with Muzak in the elevators, and goldfish in the lobby. Her ceilings were high, her walls thick, and her elegance faded.

As Kate's taxi wove in and out of traffic, carrying her to the Bauers', she thought, not of their rent, but of the apartment's layout, its convenience for a murderer. In fact, the apartment, when one came to think of it, was designed for intrusion of any sort. The entrance from the street led one into a short hall, with the Bauer apartment on one side, another doctor's office (he was not in psychiatry, Kate seemed to remember) on the other. Beyond these two entrances, the hall widened into a small lobby, with a bench, an elevator and a door beyond it to the garage. Although the main lobby of the building was stiff with attendants, this small one boasted only the elevator man who, in keeping with his kind, spent a good part of his time going up to, or down from, the upper floors. When he was in his elevator, the lobby was empty. Neither the Bauers' apartment nor the office across the hall was locked during the day. Emanuel's patients simply walked in and waited in a small waiting room until summoned by Emanuel into his office. Theoretically, if the elevator were up, one could walk in unobserved at any time.

But, of course, there would be other people about. Not to mention the other doctor and his patients and nurse, who seemed to do rather a lot of going and coming, there were Emanuel himself, his patients, possibly one in the office and one waiting, Nicola, the maid, the Bauer boys, Simon and Joshua, friends of Nicola's, friends of the boys, and of course, Kate realized, anyone living on the upper floors who had entered the building by the side entrance and waited in the small lobby for the elevator. It was becoming increasingly clear to Kate, and probably already clear to the police, that whoever had done this knew the place and the habits of the Bauers. It was a disquieting thought, but Kate refused at this point to give way to its depressing implications. Perhaps, Kate thought, the murderer had been seen. Yet in fact she doubted it. And if he or she had been seen, he or she had probably looked like a quite ordinary tenant, or visitor, or patient, and was therefore quite unmemorable, in fact invisible.

17

Kate found Nicola stretched out on her bed in the back of the apartment. Kate had walked in unnoticed by anyone except the policeman in the hall, a fact which depressed her still further, though whether she was upset by the ease of her intrusion or the presence of the policeman she could not have said. Nicola was usually to be found in the back. The Bauer living room, visible from the foyer through which the patients passed, was not used during the day or the early hours of the evening when Emanuel had patients. Great care, in fact, as all Nicola's friends knew, was taken to make sure that the patients saw no one in Emanuel's household. And even the boys had become expert at dodging back and forth between the bedroom part of the apartment and the kitchen without meeting a patient.

"Is Emanuel working?" Kate asked.

"Yes. They've let him have the office again, though of course it will be in the papers, and whether the patients will come back, or what they will think if they do, I can't imagine. I suppose actually it will bring up all sorts of fascinating material, if they care to talk about it; but it is *not* the best thing for transference during an analysis, at least not for *positive* transference, to have one's analyst's office the scene of a murder, with the analyst himself as the chief suspect. I mean, patients may have fantasies about being attacked on an analyst's couch— I'm sure most of them do—but it is best *not* to have someone actually stabbed there."

Nothing, Kate noticed thankfully, nothing could stop the flow of Nicola's talk. Except when she talked about her children (and the only way to keep from being boring on that subject, Kate believed, was to avoid it), Nicola was never dull, partly because her talk came from a joy in life that was more than egocentricity, and partly because she not only talked, she listened, listened and cared. Kate often thought that Emanuel had married Nicki largely because her language, flowing over him in waves, catching up every imaginable, every unprofound subject, buoyed him up despite the heaviness of his own mind. For the only thing which drove Emanuel eagerly to talk was an abstract idea, and, oddly, this anomaly suited them. Like most male followers of Freud, like Freud himself, if it came to that, Emanual needed and sought the company

18

of intellectual women but avoided any contractual alliance with them.

"And, of course," Nicki went on, "patients shouldn't know *anything* about their analyst, personally, and even if the police do their best—as they have promised—the papers are bound to print that he has a wife and two children, let alone is suspected of stabbing a patient on the couch, and I can't imagine how we shall ever recover from this, even if Emanuel isn't sent to jail, though they could doubtless use a brilliant psychoanalyst in jail, but if Emanuel had wanted to study the criminal mind he would have gone in for that in the first place. Perhaps if he *had*, he could figure out who did it. I keep telling him it *must* have been one of his patients, and he keeps saying, 'Let's not discuss it, Nicola,' and I'm not supposed to talk to anyone really, except perhaps Mother, who wants to rally round, but insists on looking so *brave*, but Emanuel has said I can talk to you because you know how to keep your mouth shut, and you'll be a good outlet. For me, I mean."

"Let me get you some sherry," Kate said.

"Now, don't start being sensible, or I shall scream. Pandora is being sensible with the boys; of course I am too, but I just want someone who will sit down with me and *wail*."

"I am not being sensible, merely selfish. I could use a drink myself. In the kitchen? All right, stay there, I'll get it; you plan how you can tell me all this starting right at the beginning . . ."

"I know, go on till I get to the end, and then stop. We do need the Red King, don't we? It is rather like that."

As Kate walked to the kitchen and back with the drinks, peeking first through the doors to make sure the path was clear (it would not do to meet a patient with a glass of liquor firmly grasped in each hand), Kate clarified in her own mind the sort of fact she would have to elicit from Nicki if she were to make any sense of the entire affair. She had already determined to call Reed at the D.A.'s office and blackmail him (if it should come to that) into telling her what the police knew, but meanwhile the sensible thing was to get the facts. With that odd ability to see herself from the outside, Kate noticed with interest that she had already accepted the murder as fact, that the shock had passed, that she had now reached the state where coherent action was possible.

"Well," Nicki said, sipping her sherry automatically, "it began like any other day." (Days always do, Kate thought, but we notice it only when they don't end like any other day.) "Emanuel got up with the boys. It's the only time he really gets to see them, except for odd moments during the day, and they all had breakfast together in the kitchen. Because he had an eight o'clock patient, at ten minutes of he shoved the boys into their room, where they played, though quiet play is clearly beyond them, and I continued to sleep my fitful sleep until nine . . ."

"Do you mean Emanuel has a patient at eight o'clock in the morning?"

"Of course, it's the most popular hour of all. People who work have to come either before they go to work, or in their lunch hour, or just after work at night, which is why Emanuel's day, and I suppose every psychiatrist's, stretches out so at both ends. Of course, at the moment Emanuel's got five patients in the morning, but that's a very bad arrangement, and he's planning—well, he *was* planning—to move the ten o'clock patient over to the afternoon as soon as he, the patient, could arrange his schedule to come in the afternoon. Now the eleven o'clock patient is gone, possibly to be followed by all the others."

"The eleven o'clock patient was Janet Harrison?"

"Kate, do you think she had a past? She *must* have had a past, mustn't she, if someone tracked her down and killed her in Emanuel's office? I keep pointing out that someone in analysis is very likely to mention her past, and why in hell doesn't Emanuel tell the police about her, but of course it's like the secrets of the confessional; still, the girl is dead, and Emanuel in danger . . ."

"Nicki, dear, she doesn't have to have had a past; a present will do, even a future someone wanted to avoid. I only hope whoever did it wanted to murder *her*. I mean, if the police have to find a homicidal maniac who was overcome at the sight of a girl on a couch, and who just happened to wander in, who never knew who she was—well, of course, that idea is preposterous. Let's get back to yesterday. Emanuel had patients at eight, nine, ten, eleven and twelve?"

20

"He *expected* to have; as it turned out the eleven and twelve o'clock patients canceled, or Emanuel *thought* they canceled, though of course they came, that was how I happened to find the body, because the twelve o'clock patient . . ."

"Nicki, please, let's stick to the proper order. The point is, don't leave out anything, however ordinary, however insignificant. How many patients does Emanuel have altogether, by the way; I mean, how many *did* he have, as of yesterday morning?"

"I don't know, exactly. Emanuel never talks about his work. I know he never has more than eight a day, but of course they can't all afford to come every day, so the total probably comes to ten or twelve; I don't know, you'll have to ask Emanuel."

"All right, we're up to nine o'clock yesterday morning, when you arose from your fitful sleep."

"Nine-fifteenish, really. Then the children and I make a dash for the kitchen, where I have a first breakfast, and they have a second. We tend to dawdle, actually, and usually I make lists, either of marketing I have to do, or errands of some other sort, and I telephone the butcher, and sometimes Mother, and so on. *You* know what mornings are like."

"When does Pandora come?"

"Oh, Pandora's come already. Sorry, I keep forgetting things. Pandora comes at nine; she's usually in the kitchen when I get there with the boys. After they've sampled most of my breakfast, she's stacked the dishes, and so on, she dresses the boys and they go out, unless of course it's raining. Pandora has a kind of colony she meets in the Park; I've no idea what age, or sex, or nationality the other children are, but the boys seem to like it, and Pandora, of course, is a positive monument of good sense, particularly now she's been . . ."

"It is about ten o'clock in the morning, and the children have just gone out with Pandora."

"A little after ten, actually, as a general rule. Then I begin throwing on my clothes, and so on, since I have to leave at least by twenty of eleven to get to my analytic hour, though usually I leave a bit earlier to do an errand or two on the way." Nicki, too, was in analysis, though exactly why Kate had never been able to determine.

21

It had something to do with understanding and sympathizing with her husband, but apparently Nicki had felt also a great need to work out certain problems, the chief of which seemed to be what Nicki referred to as "anxiety attacks." Kate could never discover precisely *what* an anxiety attack was, though she gathered that it was terrifying, and that its chief characteristic seemed to be the fact that there was nothing, at the time, to be anxious about. Nothing rational, that is. For example, Nicki had explained, a person might get an anxiety attack in an elevator; he would become violently anxious about the elevator's falling, but if you could *prove* to him absolutely that the elevator couldn't fall, and he might know perfectly well that it *can't*, none of that would prevent the anxiety attack. Nor, Kate had further gathered, did it mean that he (the victim of the anxiety attack) had ever been in a falling elevator, had ever known anyone who had been in a falling elevator, had ever, in fact, had anything superficially to do with elevators at all. Nicki's anxiety attacks were not associated with elevators—a pity, really, since she lived on the ground floor—but were connected, apparently, with public transportation. Not for the first time, Kate reflected that while she was impressed profoundly with the genius of Freud, the ineffectual groping, the combination of muddle and doctrine which marked clinical analysis today left her unimpressed in the extreme. The trouble was, among other things, that if Freud were to return to earth today, he would still be a better psychiatrist than anybody else; Einstein, before he died, could not understand the work then being done in physics, and this, Kate thought, was proper, and as it should be. Psychiatry, which had begun with Freud, seemed largely to have ended there; but perhaps it was too early to tell.

"Actually, I left at ten-thirty yesterday," Nicki said.

"Meanwhile, Emanuel was having patients in his office."

"Yes. In between the nine and ten o'clock patients, he came into the back of the apartment to say hello and to go to the bathroom. Everything was still all right then. I didn't see him again till . . ."

"Wait a minute, Nicki. Let's get this straight now. By ten-thirty, Emanuel was in his office with a patient (the patient, incidentally, whom he wanted to switch to the afternoon—does that possibly matter? I wonder if he knew the girl), Pandora had gone out with the children, and you were leaving for your eleven o'clock appointment and an errand. When you left, there would be no one in the apartment but Emanuel and his patient, who would be shut up in the office?"

"Yes. It sounds a bit dramatic, of course, but that's perfectly true. The police seemed very interested in all this too."

"Anyone who had observed the household would know that this is what actually happened, or what inevitably happened, unless someone was sick, or it rained?"

"Yes. But who would observe the apartment? Kate, don't you see, the whole point is precisely that."

"Nicki, please. Let's stick to the chronological report for a minute. At eleven, then, the girl, Janet Harrison, would have come; the previous patient would have left. You would be at your analyst's, the children and Pandora would be in the park, and for an hour this situation would continue?"

"For fifty minutes, anyway. The fifty-minute hour, you know. The patients leave at ten of, and the hour begins on the hour. But you see the problem the police have. I mean, one can see their point of view, even if one knows oneself that Emanuel could never have stabbed a patient in his own office, on his own couch; the whole idea is insane. There he was, or at least, they think he was, though of course he wasn't, but I mean, there they *think* he was, in a soundproof office with a girl, no one else about, and he claims that someone else came in and stabbed her on the couch and that he wasn't there at all. From their point of view, I suppose it does sound fishy, to say the least. Of course, Emanuel has told them perfectly clearly that . . ."

"Why is the room soundproofed, by the way?"

"For the patient's peace of mind, really. If a patient sitting in the waiting room should hear a sound, any sound at all, from the office, he would leap to the conclusion that *he* could be heard, and this might have dreadful inhibiting effects. So Emanuel decided to have it soundproofed—I think most psychiatrists do—and he sat in every possible place in the waiting room, while I lay on the couch in the office and screamed I LOVE MY MOTHER AND HATE MY FATHER over and over, though of course the patients don't scream, and they would never say that, but we did have to be sure, and Emanuel didn't hear a thing."

"Let's skip a minute, Nicki. Let's go on to twelve o'clock, when you found the body. Why you? Do you usually go into Emanuel's office?"

"Never during the day, really. At night I go in to dust and empty the ashtrays, since Pandora doesn't really have a chance, and in the summer sometimes, in the evenings before we go away, we sit in there because it's the only air-conditioned room in the house. But during the day none of us ever goes near it. We try even not to go back and forth too much when there's a patient in the waiting room, though Emanuel has them trained to shut the hall door behind them, so technically they couldn't see us anyway, unless they were going in or out. I know a lot of psychiatrists disapprove of an analyst having his office in his house, but they don't realize how little the patients do see of what goes on. Although Emanuel's patients probably assume he's married, only one of them has ever seen me in all these years, and he may have thought I was another patient. None of them has ever seen, I think, even an indication of the children. The office is definitely out of bounds, and I would no more go into it than I would go into Emanuel's office if it were somewhere else; probably less so."

"Suppose for some reason you have to talk to him during the day."

"If it's important, I wait till he comes back, which he often does between patients. If there is a rush, I telephone him. He has his own office phone, of course."

"But you went into the office yesterday at twelve o'clock."

"Not at twelve, no; I'm usually not home before twelve-thirty, though yesterday I was a little early. Some days I meet someone for lunch, or go downtown, and don't come home in the early afternoon at all. But yesterday, thank God—I suppose, thank God—I came home early. As I walked into the house, the twelve o'clock patient . . ."

"Did you recognize him?"

"No, of course not; I'd never seen him before. I mean, the man I later learned was the twelve o'clock patient stuck his head out the hall door and asked if the doctor was meeting his patients. It was twenty-five of one, and the doctor hadn't come to call him in. Well, you know, Kate, that was extremely odd. Emanuel has never in his life stood up a patient. I knew he had had an eleven o'clock patient (Janet Harrison), and he never tries to dash out in the ten minutes between patients. I wondered what could have happened to him. Could he be in his office, feeling, for some reason, unable to meet a patient? I dialed his office phone from the telephone in the kitchen, and after three rings, the service answered, so I knew he wasn't there, or wasn't answering, and then I became worried. Meanwhile, I'd coaxed the patient back into the waiting room. Of course, I was having all sorts of fantasies about his having had a heart attack in the office, or having been unable to get rid of the eleven o'clock patient— one does have the oddest fantasies at these times—Pandora was in the kitchen with the boys getting lunch, and I went and knocked on the office door. I knew the patient in the waiting room was aware of what I was doing, though he couldn't see me, but I had to do something, and naturally, no one answered the knock, so I opened the door a bit and stuck my head in. She was right there on the couch, which is near the door; I couldn't possibly miss seeing her. At first I thought, She's fallen asleep, but then I saw the knife sticking out of her chest. And Emanuel nowhere to be found. I did have the presence of mind to close the office door and tell the patient he'd better go. He was curious, and clearly reluctant to leave a scene which he sensed was fraught with drama, but I ushered him out. I was extremely calm, as one often is right after a shock."

"And then you sent for the police?"

"No. Actually I never thought of the police, not then."

"What *did* you do?"

"I rushed into the office across the hall and got the doctor. He was very nice and came right away, even though he had an office full of patients. His name is Barrister, Michael Barrister. He told me she was dead."

chapter 3

"Dinner seems to be served," said Emanuel, coming into the bedroom. "Hello, Kate. Pandora has set a place for you. How that woman carries on like this, I don't know, but she has never had any use for the police."

"You carry on fairly well yourself," Kate said.

"Today, after all, was still a bit of the old life for me. The patients didn't know yet, at least not till the last one at six o'clock. He had an evening paper."

"Do the papers mention it?" Nicola asked.

"Mention it! I'm afraid at the moment we *are* the news. Pyschiatry, couches, female patients, male doctors, knives —one can scarcely blame them. Let's say good night to the boys and have some dinner."

But it was not until dinner was over, and they were in the living room, that they talked again of the murder. Kate had half expected Emanuel to disappear, but he seemed to want to talk. Usually some inner need to "get something done," to "make use of time," either drove him from social occasions, or subjected him, if he remained, to the pressure of a mounting inner tension. Yet tonight, with a real problem looming, as it were, in the external world, Emanuel seemed, almost with thankfulness, to have relaxed in the contemplation of something beyond his control. The very externality of the murder gave him a kind of relief. Kate, recognizing this, knew the police would mistake his calm for some symptom, some indication of guilt, when in fact, if they only knew, it was the assurance of his innocence. Had he murdered the girl, the problem would not, of course, have been outside. Yet what policeman in the world could one convince of all this? Stern? Kate forced her thoughts back to the facts.

"Emanuel," she asked, "where were you between ten

of eleven and twelve-thirty? Don't tell me you suffered a blow on the head and simply wandered about, uncertain of who you were."

Emanuel looked at her, and then at Nicola, and said to Kate, "How much has she told you?"

"Only the normal routine of the day, really, plus a word or two on the finding of the body. We had, for the moment, skipped over the magic hour."

"Magic is the word," Emanuel said. "It was all done with such cleverness that really, you know, I don't blame the police for suspecting me; I almost suspect myself. When you add to the quite justified suspicions of police, the mysterious and still, I fear, not quite fully American profession of psychiatry, it's no wonder they assume that I went mad and stabbed the girl on my couch. I don't think they have any doubts."

"Why haven't they arrested you?"

"I wondered that myself, and decided finally that there really isn't, yet, quite enough evidence. I don't know much about the ins and outs of this, but I gather the D.A.'s office has to be convinced they've got enough evidence to have a good chance for conviction before they'll allow an arrest and trial. A really clever lawyer (which it is assumed I could afford with ease) would make mincemeat of what they've got so far. As I see it, there are two problems: what this will do to me professionally, which I prefer for the moment to ignore, and the fact that as long as they believe I did it they will not really work to find who did. In that case I am doomed, either way."

Kate felt a great surge of admiration and affection for this deeply intelligent and honest man. No one knew better than she (or, perhaps, did Nicola?) his failure to meet the day-to-day demands of a personal relationship, but at that still center of himself she recognized, as in every crisis she always would, an honor, an identity, that nothing would shatter. She had lived long enough to know that when you find intelligence and integrity in the same individual, you have found a prize.

"I'm surprised they let you go on seeing your patients, even today," said Nicola, in tones of sarcasm. "Perhaps you might go mad, since we are apparently to consider it a symptom of your profession, and stab another victim. Wouldn't they look foolish then?"

27

"On the contrary," Kate said lightly. "They'd have their case wrapped up. I imagine that partly they are hoping he will do it again, and cast away all doubt, and partly even they, in their dim, methodical way, suspect somewhere in the depths of their beings that Emanuel didn't do it." Her eyes met Emanuel's and then dropped, but he had seen the faith, and it had strengthened him.

"The irony great enough to make Shakespeare howl," Emanuel said, "is that the girl had recently become very angry, which means transference. When she canceled today, I assumed it was because of that, and didn't feel surprised. How clever we like to think we are!"

"Did she call you to cancel the appointment?"

"I didn't speak to her, but in the normal course of events that is hardly surprising. She and the twelve o'clock patient—who later showed up and catapulted Nicki into finding the body—both of them, I learned at about five of eleven, had canceled their appointments."

"Isn't that a bit unusual?"

"Not really. As a rule, of course, two patients don't cancel in a row, but it's by no means extraordinary. Sometimes patients hit a patch of difficult material, and just can't face it for a while. It happens in the course of every analysis. Or they tell themselves they're too tired, or too busy, or too upset. Freud came to understand this very early. It's one of the reasons we insist on charging patients for canceled appointments, even where they appear to have, do have, a perfectly legitimate excuse. People who don't understand psychiatry are always shocked and think we are moneygrubbers, but the whole mechanism of paying, and even sacrificing to pay for an analysis, is an important part of the therapy."

"How did you learn at five of eleven that they had both canceled?"

"I called the exchange and they told me."

"The exchange is the answering service? Do you call them every hour?"

"Not unless I know there's been a call."

"You mean while you were in there with a patient, the phone rang, and you didn't answer it?"

"The phone doesn't ring; it has a yellow light which flashes on and off instead of a ring. The patient can't see it from the couch. If I don't answer after three rings, or

28

three flashes, the exchange answers. Of course, I don't interrupt patients by answering the phone."

"Did you find out who spoke to the exchange to cancel the appointments? Was it a man and a woman, or a man for both, or what?"

"I thought of that, of course, first thing, but when I got to the exchange someone else was on duty, and they don't keep any record of the voice they spoke to, merely the message and the time. Doubtless the police will look into it more carefully."

Nicola, who had been sitting quietly during this exchange, whirled around to face Kate. "Before you ask another question, let me ask you something. This is the part that sticks in the throats of the police; I know it is, but maybe Emanuel has talked to enough people about it so that they'll find out it's probably true, and anyway we've met other psychiatrists who do the same things because they feel so shut up."

"Nicki, dear," Kate said, "not to mention your pronouns, I haven't an idea in the world what you're talking about."

"Of course not; I haven't asked you the question yet. Here it is: If a patient of Emanuel's canceled, what would Emanuel do?"

"Go somewhere. No matter where, just go."

"You see," Nicola said. "Everyone knows that. I'd guess you'd go down to Brentano's to browse among the paper books, and my mother, when I asked her that question, decided he'd think of an errand, somewhere, he simply had to do, but the important point is that the police cannot understand that a psychiatrist, who must sit quietly all day listening, relaxes by moving. They think if he wasn't harboring nefarious plans, he would have stayed nicely in his office like any other sane person, catching up on his correspondence. At his *most* abandoned, they are convinced he would have called up a friend and had lunch downtown with two vodka cocktails first. It's no good telling them that Emanuel never eats lunch, *certainly* never eats it with anyone else, and in any case is not geared to calling people up for lunch because he's never, except for a fluke like this—and now that I think of it, it isn't a fluke, it was planned—free for lunch."

"What did you do, Emanuel?" Kate asked.

"I walked around the reservoir; round and round and round, at a kind of trot."

"I know; I've seen you; I've trotted too." It had been long ago, before Nicola, when she was still young enough to run just for the hell of it.

"It was spring; the spring was in my blood." Kate thought of the chalk inscription. She seemed to have viewed it in another lifetime. She was suddenly dog tired, and felt herself collapse, like one of those cartoon figures she remembered from her childhood who discovered they were sitting on nothing, and then fell to the floor. From the first emotional shock of Detective Stern's announcement—*She has been murdered*—until this moment, she had allowed no feeling to cluster about the idea of Emanuel's situation. Particularly, she had excluded from her attention the question of responsibility for this situation. She was sufficiently logical, even in this state of emotional and physical exhaustion, not to hold herself wholly to blame. She could not have known the girl would be murdered, could not have guessed—indeed, could not have imagined—that she would be murdered in Emanuel's office. Had such an idea crossed her mind, Kate would have decided that, in Nicola's language, she was "hallucinating."

Yet if Kate was no more than a single link in the chain of events which had led to this disaster, she had, nonetheless, a responsibility, not only to Emanuel and Nicola, but to herself, perhaps also to Janet Harrison.

"Do you remember that joke of a few years ago?" she said to them, "the one about the two psychiatrists on the stairs, and one of them gooses the other. The goosed one is at first rather angry, and then, shrugging his shoulders, dismisses the incident. 'After all,' he is supposed to have said, 'it's *his* problem.' Well, I can't do the same; it's my problem too, even if you were not my friends."

From the way in which Emanuel and Nicola avoided looking at each other, or at her, she knew this point had been at least mentioned between them. "In fact," she continued, "regarded in a certain light, shall we say the light of the police, I'm a rather nice suspect myself. The detective who came to see me asked what I was doing yesterday morning. It may have been what they call 'routine'; it may not."

Emanuel and Nicola stared at her. "That's absolute nonsense," Emanuel said.

"No more nonsense, really, than that you should have murdered her in your own office, or that Nicola might have. Look at it from Detective Stern's point of view: I know the routine, more or less, of your household and office. As it happens, I didn't know about your telephone, about its lighting up instead of ringing, or about your not answering when a patient is there, but there's only my word for that. I sent the girl to Emanuel. Perhaps I was madly jealous of her, or had stolen her money, or one of her literary ideas, and seized the chance to kill her."

"But you didn't have any personal connection with her, did you?" Nicola asked.

"Of course I didn't. But neither, I assume, did Emanuel. Yet the police must suppose there was some connection, a mad passion or something of the sort, if he was going to kill her in his office. I don't imagine they suppose he went off his head all of a sudden, and stabbed her in the middle of one of her more interesting free associations."

"She was very beautiful," Nicola said. She dropped the sentence, like an awkward gift from a child, into their laps. Both Emanuel and Kate started to say "How do you know?" Neither of them said it. Could Nicki have noticed the girl was beautiful in the moment when she saw her dead? With a shock, Kate remembered the girl's beauty. It had not been of the flamboyant sort toward which men turned their heads on the street, around which they clustered at a party. That sort of beauty, as like as not, is the result of startling coloring, and a certain pleasing symmetry of the face. Janet Harrison had had what Kate called beauty in the bones. The finely chiseled features, the planes of the face, the deep-set eyes, the broad, clear forehead—these made her beauty which, at the second or third look, suddenly presented itself as though it had been in hiding. *My God*, Kate thought, remembering, *it needed only that*. "The point I was going to make," she went on after a moment, "is that I feel a responsibility for all this, a guilt if you will, and if nothing else you will certainly be helping me if you allow me to get everything that happened, as far as you know it, straight in my mind. I see fairly clearly how the day went. At ten-thirty Nicola

31

had left, and Emanuel was in his office with the ten o'clock patient when the phone light flashed to indicate a call. Did it flash once, I mean for just one call, or twice?"

"Twice. Obviously, even if it was the same person—shall we say the murderer—calling to cancel, falsely, for both of them, he would take the trouble to call twice. It would immediately be suspicious if one person called to cancel two patients. The patients don't even know each other."

"Do you know that they don't?"

"Let me put it this way. They may have met casually in the waiting room; it does sometimes happen. But if they knew each other at all well, I would probably know it."

"It would come up in the analysis?" Emanuel nodded, obviously unwilling to discuss this in detail. "But," Kate asked, "if the twelve o'clock patient, who was a man, wanted, for some reason, to keep her attraction for him, her connection with him secret, wouldn't he do so?"

"It would be unexpected."

"And," Kate added, "might indicate that he had been planning to murder her." No one had any answer to that. "Well, to continue, at ten to eleven you called the service, and they told you of the two cancellations. So you immediately left the office and went to run around the reservoir."

"You see," Nicola interrupted, "you believe that's what he did, and yet it sounds crazy even when you say it."

Emanuel smiled, that half-smile of his which indicated his acceptance of the inevitable. It occurred to Kate that Emanuel was able, more than anyone she knew, to accept the inevitable. It was something, perhaps, for which psychiatry trained you, a profession of few surprises to one well and long trained in it. Could Janet Harrison's murder possibly be considered a professional surprise? Kate tucked that bone away, to be gnawed on later. "I didn't leap from the chair out to the reservoir," Emanuel said. "I may want exercise, but not that impetuously. I went to the back of the apartment and changed my clothes. Then I wandered out in what I think could be called a leisurely fashion."

"Did anyone see you go? Did you meet anyone?"

"No one who can swear to it. The hall was empty."

Nicola sat up. "Perhaps one of Dr. Barrister's patients saw him go by the window, toward Fifth Avenue. I'm sure if we asked him, he'd be willing to ask them, in a matter of this importance. Or he might have seen you from his office."

"It's unlikely; anyway, even if they had, or he had, there's no reason, from the police's point of view, why I couldn't have doubled back. And I didn't meet anyone going around the reservoir. At least, I passed some people, but I can't remember *them*. How could they identify a man in dirty pants and an old jacket, walking fast?"

"You were wearing those clothes when you came back," Nicola said. "Surely you wouldn't have been wearing them during her analysis. Doesn't that prove you didn't murder her?"

"He could have changed them after he stabbed her," Kate said. "But wait a minute. If you're supposed to have planned your own alibi, if you can call trotting around the reservoir an alibi, who is supposed to have made the two calls canceling the patients? You said the answering service records the time. If you were with a patient, and you were, you couldn't have made the calls. Even if the patient didn't see the flashing lights—and the murderer may have known that—the answering service would know when the calls were received."

"I've thought of that," Emanuel said. "I even went so far as to point it out to the police, though that may not have been very wise of me. They made no comment, but undoubtedly their point will be that I could have paid someone to make the calls for me, or got Nicki to, or you."

"It's still a weak point in their case. Personally, I intend to clasp it firmly to my bosom. Why, by the way, do you suppose the murderer made the calls then, and not while you were in your office alone? Then there really would be no one's word for it but yours."

"Perhaps he was unable to make them at another time. More likely, though, he wanted to be sure that I *would not* answer the phone and take the messages. I might recognize that these were not my patients' voices, or—though this seems unlikely—I might have recognized the voice on the phone."

"There's another possibility too," Nicola said. "If he called earlier, even you, with your great drive to go run

33

around, *might* have had time to plan something else. You might, for instance, have mentioned it to me, and I might have said: Goody, now we can both sit down and figure out the budget, or make love—that is, of course, if I canceled *my* analytic hour, I know it's unlikely, but anyone who knows us as well as this murderer does might know I was just the sort to do something like that. With Pandora out, I might have decided how nice, for a change, to go to bed together in the morning—I don't think he or she wanted to give Emanuel time to think, and he wanted to make sure I was gone."

"All the same," Kate said, "it may be a slip, and a bad one. Let's hope so. When you came home, Emanuel, the curtain, so to speak, had gone up?"

"Chaos had come would be a better way to describe it. If one weren't concerned oneself, it might even have been interesting."

"Dr. Barrister told me I had better call the police," Nicola said. "He even seemed to know the number, Spring something, but I couldn't seem to dial, I just picked up the phone to dial operator, so he took the phone and dialed the number. Then he handed it back to me. A man's voice said 'Police Department,' and I thought, This is all a fantasy. I shall tell Dr. Sanders about it tomorrow. I wonder what it indicates. It couldn't have been even a minute later, I suppose, they radioed to one of those cars policemen are always riding around in—do you remember when we were children, policemen used to walk?"

"When we were children," Emanuel put in, "policemen used to be old men. What is it someone said? They're old enough to be your father, and suddenly, one day, they're young enough to be your son."

"Anyway," Nicola continued, "these ordinary policemen just looked at the body, as though to make sure we weren't pulling their leg, though it seems an odd sort of joke to me, and then *they* called in, and the next thing we knew, the parade had started; men with all kinds of equipment, and detectives, and someone called a deputy inspector, people taking photographs, a funny little man they all greeted with great joy as the 'M.E.'. I really lost track of all of them. We were sitting here in the living room. I don't remember when Emanuel came back, but it seemed a long time before they carried her out.

34

The only thing I really noticed was that an ambulance came, with some men in white, and one of them said to one of the policemen, 'It's D.O.A., all right.' I saw a movie once called *D.O.A.* It means Dead on Arrival. Whose arrival?"

"They seemed very interested to see me when I returned, needless to say," Emanuel went on. "But I had to sit down and cancel my afternoon patients. I couldn't reach all of them, and one of them was turned away by a policeman, which I didn't care for, but perhaps it was better than if I had come out in the middle of all that and told her to go. At any rate, 'chaos' is the word. How efficient the police are, and how little they understand!"

Later that night the words echoed in Kate's mind: *How little they understand!* Shortly after Emanuel had uttered the words, a detective had come again to talk to them. He had let Kate go, after a long look. Yet, Kate thought, putting herself wearily to bed, the facts, if they were facts, on Emanuel's side were not the sort the police, who must all have stanch lower-middle-class backgrounds, could understand: that a psychiatrist, though he might be more driven than other men, would never commit a crime in his office, on the grounds, so to speak, of his profession; that Emanuel would never entangle himself with a woman patient, however beautiful; that Emanuel could never murder anyone, certainly not stab them with a knife; that a man and woman who had been lovers, she and Emanuel, could now be friends. What could the police make of that, the police who knew, probably, only sex on one hand, and marriage on the other. What of Nicola? "She was very beautiful," Nicola had said. But surely Nicola was at her analysis, the perfect alibi.

As the two sleeping pills which Kate had taken—and she had not taken sleeping pills since a horrible case of poison ivy, seven years ago—began to pull her under, she concentrated her weakening attention on the doctor across the hall. Obviously, the murderer. The fact, and it was a fact, that he was without the smallest connection with anyone in the case, seemed, as consciousness faded, to be of very little importance.

chapter 4

REED AMHEARST was an Assistant District Attorney, though exactly what functions were encompassed by that title, Kate had never understood. Apparently he was frequently in court, and found his work exciting and consuming. He and Kate had stumbled across each other years before, in the short period of political activity in Kate's life, when she had worked for a reform political club. Politics had been for Reed a more continuous affair, but after Kate had retired, exhausted from her first and only primary fight, she and Reed continued to see each other in a friendly sort of way. They had dinner together, or went to the theater from time to time, and laughed together a good deal. When either of them needed a partner for a social evening, and did not wish for some reason to plunge in with any other attachment, Reed or Kate, as the case might be, would go along. Since neither of them had married, since neither of them could have considered, for a single moment, the completely outrageous idea of marrying each other, their casual acquaintance became a constant amid all the variables of their social lives.

So they might have continued indefinitely, eventually tottering, occasionally together, into benign old age, if Reed, through a series of impulses and bad judgments, had not landed himself in a most magnificent muddle. The details of this Kate had long since forgotten, believing that the ability to forget was one of the most important requirements of a friendship, but neither of them could ever forget that it was Kate who had got him out of the muddle, rescued him on the brink of disaster. By doing so, she had put him forever in her debt, but Reed was a nice enough person to accept a service without holding it against the giver. To ask for a repayment of the debt was an abhorrent idea, to Kate, and to call on him now would, she could not but realize, put her in the position of seeming to do exactly that. For this reason, despite her resolutions of the day before, she brooded a full two hours the next morning before calling him.

On the other hand, however, and equally imperious, was the need to help Emanuel. No one, Kate was convinced, could help Emanuel, unless he combined her belief in Emanuel's innocence with the knowledge of the police. The only possible way to get that knowledge seemed to be through Reed. Cursing her mind, too finely tuned to moral dilemmas which more sensible people happily ignored, cursing Reed for having ever needed her help, she decided, after two aspirins, eight cups of coffee and much pacing of the living room, to ask his help. It was, at least, a Thursday, thus a classless day. With a lingering thought for her innocent Tuesday morning in the stacks—would she ever return to Thomas Carlyle, abandoned in the midst of one of his older perorations?—she picked up the phone.

She caught Reed just as he was leaving on some pressing mission. He had, of course, heard of the "body on the couch," as they appeared to be calling it (Kate suppressed a groan). When he gathered what she wanted—the complete dossier (if they used that word) on the case—he was absolutely silent for perhaps twenty seconds; it seemed an hour. "Good friend of yours?" he asked.

"Yes," Kate answered, "and in a hell of an unfair mess," and then cursed herself for appearing to be reminding him. But what the hell, she thought, I am reminding him; it does no good to pussyfoot around it.

"I'll do what I can," he said. (Obviously he was not alone.) "It looks like a bad day, but I'll look into the matter for you and report to your apartment about seven-thirty tonight. Will that do?" Well, after all, Kate thought, he works for a living. Did you expect him to come dashing up the minute he replaced the receiver? He's probably making a huge effort as it is.

"I'll be waiting for you, Reed; thanks a lot." She hung up the phone.

For the first time in years, Kate found herself at loose ends, not delightful loose ends, at which one says: If I

37

look at another student theme I shall be ill, and sneaks off, surreptitiously, to a movie; this rather was the horrible kind of loose ends, to which Kate had heard applied (always with a shudder) the cure of "killing time." Her life was full enough of varied activity to make leisure seem a blessing, not a burden, but now she found herself wondering what in the world to do until seven-thirty. She nobly fought the urge to call Emanuel and Nicola; it seemed best to wait until she had something constructive to say. Work was impossible—she found she could neither prepare a class nor correct papers. After a certain amount of aimless wandering about the apartment—and she felt, irrationally, that it was a fort she was holding, which she must not on any account leave—she applied the remedy her mother had used under stress, when Kate was a child: she cleaned closets.

This task, combining as it did dirt, hard work and amazed discovery, lasted her nicely until two o'clock. Exhausted, she then abandoned the hall closet to dust and unaccountable accumulation, and collapsed in a chair with Freud's *Studies in Hysteria,* a Christmas present from Nicola several years back. She could not concentrate, but one sentence caught her eye, a comment of Freud's to a patient: "Much will be gained if we succeed in transforming your hysterical misery into common unhappiness." She wished she had had it to quote to Emanuel when they had still been free to argue, aimlessly, about Freud. No wonder they had such a hard row to hoe, these modern psychoanalysts: they saw little enough hysterical misery, and were left to cope with common unhappiness, for which, as Freud clearly knew, there is no clinical cure. It occurred to her that her aim now was to assist, if she could, in restoring Emanuel to common unhappiness from the catastrophic fate which seemed to face him. A disquieting thought, from which she passed into idle daydreams.

How the rest of the afternoon passed she never, afterward, could tell. She straightened up the house, took a shower—guiltily lifting the phone off the hook first so that a possible caller (Nicola, Reed, the police?) would get a busy signal and try again—ordered some groceries in case Reed should be hungry, and paced back and forth. Several telephone conversations with people who never mentioned murders or had anything to do with them helped considerably.

At twenty-five of eight Reed came. Kate had to restrain herself from greeting him like the long-lost heir from overseas. He collapsed into a chair and gladly accepted Scotch and water.

"I suppose your idea is that the psychiatrist didn't do it?"

"Of course he didn't do it," Kate said; "the idea is preposterous."

"My dear, the idea that a friend of yours could commit murder may be preposterous; I'll be the first to admit that it is, or to take your word for it in any case. But to the minds of the police, beautifully unsullied with any personal preconceptions, he looks as guilty as a sinner in hell. All right, all right, don't argue with me yet; I'll give you the facts, and then you can tell me what a lovely soul he has, and who the real criminal is, if any."

"Reed! Is there a chance she could have done it herself?"

"Not a chance, really, though I'll admit a good defense lawyer might make something of the idea in court, just to confuse the minds of the jury. People who thrust a knife deep into their innards don't thrust upward, and certainly don't do it on their backs; they throw themselves on the blade, like Dido. If they do thrust a knife into themselves, they bare that portion of their body— don't ask me why, they always do, or so it says in the textbook—and, a less debatable point, they inevitably leave fingerprints on the knife."

"Perhaps she was wearing gloves."

"Then she removed them after death."

"Maybe someone else removed them."

"Kate, dear, I think I had better make you a drink; possibly you should take it with several tranquilizers. They are said, together with alcohol, to have a stultifying effect on one's reactions. Shall we stick for the moment to the facts?" Kate, fetching herself the drink and a cigarette, but not the tranquilizers, nodded obediently. "Good. She was killed between ten of eleven, when the ten o'clock patient left, and twelve thirty-five, when she was discovered by Mrs. Bauer, and the discovery noted, more or less, by Dr. Michael Barrister, Pandora

39

Jackson and Frederick Sparks, the twelve o'clock patient. The Medical Examiner won't estimate the death any closer than that—they never estimate closer than within two hours—but he has said, strictly unofficially, which means he won't testify to it in court, that she was probably killed almost an hour before she was found. There was no external bleeding, because the hilt of the knife, where it joins the blade, pressed her clothing into the wound, preventing the escape of any blood. This is unfortunate, since a bloodstained criminal, with bloodstained clothes, is that much easier to find." Reed's voice was colorless and totally without emotion, like the voice of a stenographer reading back from notes. Kate was grateful to him.

"She was killed," he continued, "with a long, thin carving knife from the Bauer kitchen, one of a set that hangs in a wooden holder on the wall. The Bauers do not deny their ownership of the knife, which is just as well, since it bears both their fingerprints." Involuntarily, Kate gasped. Reed paused to look at her. "I can see," he said wryly, "that your ability to differentiate between sorts of evidence is not very developed. That's the chief evidence on their side. Since every tot today knows about fingerprints, the chances are that, using the knife as a weapon, they would have had the brains to remove them. Of course, a trained psychiatrist of admitted brilliance might have been smart enough to figure that the police would figure that way. Don't interrupt. Dr. and Mrs. Bauer say their prints got on the knife the previous night when they had a small argument about how to carve a silver-tip roast, and both gave it a try. Being sensible people, they don't submerge knives in water, but wipe off the blade with a damp cloth and then a dry one. The prints, if anything, are evidence in their favor, since they have been partially obliterated, as they might have been if someone had held the knife with gloves. This, however, is inconclusive.

"Now we come to the more damning part. She was stabbed while she was lying down, according to the medical evidence, by someone who leaned over the end of the couch and over her head, and thrust the knife upward between her ribs. This seems, incidentally, to have been done by someone with a fairly developed knowledge of anatomy, *id est*, a doctor, but here again we are on shaky ground. This particular upward thrust of the knife

40

from behind (though not with the victim lying down) was commonly taught to all resistance units during World War II in France and elsewhere. The important question is, Who could have got the girl to lie down, Who could have got behind her, Who could have finally stabbed her without at any point inspiring any resistance whatever? You can see that the police are saying to themselves: 'Where does a psychoanalyst sit? In a chair behind the head of a patient.' Detective: 'Why does the psychoanalyst sit there, Dr. Bauer?' Dr. Bauer: 'So that the patient cannot see the doctor.' Detective: 'Why shouldn't the patient see the doctor?' Dr. Bauer: 'That's a very interesting question; there are many possible explanations, such as helping the patient to maintain the anonymity of the doctor, thus increasing the possibilities for transference; but the real reason seems to be that Freud invented the position because he could not bear to have the patients looking at him all day long.' Detective: 'Do all your patients lie on the couch?' Dr. Bauer: 'Only those in analysis; patients in therapy sit in a chair on the other side of the desk.' Detective: 'Do you sit behind them?' Dr. Bauer: 'No.' Shrug of detective's shoulders not reported here."

"Reed, do you mean the police are basing their whole case on the fact that no one else could have got behind her while she was lying on the couch?"

"Not quite, but it is a sticky point, all the same. If Dr. Bauer wasn't there, why was she lying down on the couch in the first place? And, assuming for the moment that she wandered into the room and lay down when there was no one there—and Dr. Bauer has assured the detective that no patient would do any such thing, they wait until they are summoned into the office by the analyst —would she continue to lie there if someone other than the analyst walked in, sat down behind her, and then leaned over her with a knife?"

"Supposedly she didn't see the knife when he leaned over?"

"Even so. And if the analyst wasn't there, why did she lie down on the couch? Why do women lie down on couches? All right, you needn't answer that."

"Wait a minute, Reed. Perhaps she wanted to take a nap."

"Come off it, Kate."

"All right, but suppose she was in love with one of the patients before or after her—we don't really know anything about them—and she, or one of them, let's say one of them, got rid of Emanuel so that he and the girl could make love on the couch. After all, the ten o'clock patient would simply stay, and the twelve o'clock patient *did* come rather early . . ."

"Those two cancellations were made during the ten o'clock patient's hour, so he could hardly have made them himself."

"Exactly. He got someone else to do it. It gave him an alibi, and since he was there at the time himself, he could make sure that the calls came through, or at least that *some* calls came through."

"Then why cancel *for* the twelve o'clock patient, and not cancel the twelve o'clock patient as well? All right, perhaps he didn't know his phone number. But then why try to get rid of Dr. Bauer, when you will have the twelve o'clock patient walking in on you anyway?"

"To lovers an hour alone together is an eternity," said Kate in sepulchral tones. "Besides, he really didn't want to make love; he wanted to murder her."

"I'll say this, you have an answer for everything. Might I point out, however, that you have created this whole plot out of thin air? There isn't the smallest evidence for anything you've said, though the police will, I'm sure, try to collect the evidence wherever possible."

"If only I were as sure of that as you are. There isn't a shred of evidence against Emanuel either."

"Kate, my dear, I admire your loyalty to Emanuel, but do exercise your extraordinary ability to face the facts: the girl was murdered in Emanuel's office, with Emanuel's knife, in a position that would have given Emanuel every opportunity to commit the crime. He can provide no alibi; while the phone calls canceling the patients were undoubtedly made, he as well as anyone else could have paid someone to make them. The murder was done when no one else was in the apartment, but who except Emanuel and his wife *knew* that no one else would be in the apartment? Despite your delightful flights of fancy, we don't *know* that the girl knew a single other person connected with that office. In fact, one of the strangest things about

42

this case is how little they seem able to find out about that girl."

"Was she a virgin?"

"No idea; she never had a child, at any rate."

"Reed! Do you mean to tell me that when they do one of these autopsies they can't tell whether or not a girl's a virgin? I thought that was one of the first things they reported on."

"It is remarkable, the old wives' tales that continue to be believed by otherwise quite intelligent people. The point of this tale, I suppose, is to keep girls good. How did you suppose one could tell? If you are thinking of what the Elizabethans alluded to so feelingly as 'maidenhead,' I am sad to report that the number of modern girls who survive their athletic girlhoods with that intact is tiny enough to make your grandmother blush. Otherwise, what evidence did you suppose there was? If semen is present, we know a woman has had sexual relations; if she is bruised or torn, we suspect rape, or attempted rape. Nothing like this, of course, was in evidence here. But, as to whether or not she was a virgin, you would do better asking the people who knew her, if you can find them."

"I cannot remember when I have been so shocked. The world as I knew it is fast passing away."

"Your friend Emanuel can probably tell you if she has had sexual relations, that is, if you can get him to tell you anything."

"Since the police, completely ignoring Emanuel's character, are convinced he did it, what do they suppose was his motive?"

"The police are not so interested in motive; good sound circumstantial evidence is much more their cup of tea. They pay it due attention, of course, and if one of those two patients turns out to inherit a million dollars under Janet Harrison's will, they'll prick up their ears. But a doctor who has become entangled with a beautiful patient and decided in a rash moment to get rid of her is motive enough for them."

"But they have no evidence that he was 'entangled' with her; that's probably why they haven't arrested him yet. Whereas I have loads of evidence that he couldn't have become entangled with her, couldn't have murdered her, and certainly not on his couch."

43

"All right, I want to hear it all. First, let me give you the rest. The thrust of the knife which killed her was delivered with a good deal of strength, but not with more than a strongish woman might have mustered—you for instance, or Mrs. Bauer. Let me finish. The body was not moved after being stabbed, but I've already told you that. No signs of a struggle. No fingerprints, other than those one would expect. The rest is a lot of technical jargon, including photographs of a particularly sickening nature. We come now to the only real point of interest.

"The murderer—we assume it was the murderer—went through her purse, presumably after she was dead. He was wearing rubber gloves, which leave their own peculiar sort of print, in this case on the gold-colored clasp of her pocketbook. The supposition is that if he found something, he took it out. The girl was not very well known to those who lived near her in the Graduate Women's Dormitory at the university, but one of them, questioned by the police, had noticed that Janet Harrison always carried a notebook in her purse; no notebook was found there. Also, she appeared to have no photographs in her purse or wallet, though almost every woman does carry photographs of someone or other. That is all conjecture. But there *was* a picture which the murderer apparently missed. In her wallet she had a New York driver's license, not the new card sort, but the old paper kind which folded, and folded inside it was a small picture of a young man. The police are of course going to try to discover who he was; I'll get a copy of it shortly and let you see it, just in case it rings a bell. The important point is that she had carefully concealed the picture. Why?"

"It sounds as though she thought someone might go through her pocketbook, and she didn't want the picture found. Some people, of course, are naturally secretive."

"Apparently Miss Harrison was *un*naturally secretive. Nobody seems to have known her very well. There is some information from the university, but it's pretty thin. Oddly enough, her room in the Graduate Women's Hall was robbed the night before her death, though whether this is a coincidence or not we may never know. Someone apparently had a key, rifled through everything, and departed with a 35-millimeter camera worth about seventy dollars. A brand new Royal portable typewriter, worth more, was left, whether because it was too conspicuous to carry out, or the robber was collecting only cameras, it is impossible to determine. All her drawers, and her desk, were thoroughly rifled, but apparently nothing else was taken. It was reported to the local precinct, but, though they conscientiously made out a report, this sort of thing is pretty hopeless. By the time she had been murdered, the room had been straightened out, so any evidence that may have been left is gone.

"The information on Janet Harrison is surprisingly meager, though we haven't traced her back home yet; the police in North Dakota, where she turns out, surprisingly enough, to come from, are finding what they can. All the university can tell us is that she is thirty years of age . . ."

"*Really?*" Kate said. "She didn't look it."

"Apparently not. She's a U.S. citizen, and went to college at some place called Collins. The university noticed that the 'person to notify in case of emergency' section was not filled out, and the omission apparently went unnoticed in the rush of registration. That's about it, I think," Reed finished up, "except for one little matter I've saved, with my well known flair for the dramatic, till the end: Nicola Bauer wasn't at her analyst's the morning of the murder. She called up at the last minute to cancel the appointment. The police have just managed to reach her analyst. She claims to have spent the morning wandering in the park, not around the reservoir, but near something she calls the old castle. People do, of course, spend a remarkable amount of innocent time wandering about, but that *both* of the Bauers should have ambled separately around Central Park while someone was being murdered in their apartment is difficult for the Deputy Inspector wholly to believe. With all the good will in the world, I can't help seeing his point."

Reed got up, and very kindly poured Kate another drink. "Just keep in mind, please, Kate, that they may have done it. I don't say they did; I don't say I shan't sympathize with your conviction that they didn't; I'll help you any way I can. But, please, as a favor to me, keep in the back of your mind an awareness of the possibility that they may be guilty. Janet Harrison was a very beautiful girl."

45

chapter 5

KATE had met Emanuel at a time when they had both gone stale, when the world seemed to each flat and unprofitable, if not out of joint. They happened, in fact, to meet at that identical point in their lives when each was committed to a career, but had not yet admitted the commitment. Their meeting had been the one romantic (in the movie sense) moment in both their lives, and though Kate may have been what Emanuel was later to call "projecting," it seemed to her even then that they both realized they had met dramatically, because destined to meet, that they were further destined never to marry, never wholly to part.

They had crashed into each other, literally, on an exit road from the Merritt Parkway. Kate, as she was soon to point out to him, was exiting in the proper fashion, as anyone might be expected to do. Emanuel, quite on the contrary, was backing up the exit road toward the Parkway from which he had just mistakenly emerged. It was dusk; Kate's mind was on the directions she had to follow, Emanuel's, still seething, was apparently not functioning at all. It was a very pretty crash.

They ended up, after a certain amount of expostulation which soon turned to laughter, driving to a restaurant in Emanuel's car, from which they telephoned for aid for Kate's car. They both forgot that they were expected elsewhere, Emanuel because, as Nicola was later to say, forgetting was his favorite sport, and Kate deliberately because she did not want her hosts to come for her. She had not "fallen in love" with Emanuel; she would never be "in love" with him. But she wanted to stay with him that evening.

Walking now to Emanuel's home, with Reed's warning of the night before still ringing in her ears, Kate thought how difficult it would be (might turn out to be) to explain their relationship to a policeman. She was walking from Riverside Drive to Fifth Avenue in the hope that the exercise and air might clear her head, and it occurred to her that even this act might seem, to certain people, inexplicable. Suppose someone were murdered now in her apartment; what sort of alibi would it be, the simple statement that she had decided to walk halfway across the city? True, Emanuel and Nicola, whose alibis were similar to this, had not had a destination, but had been seized with an unaccountable desire to wander; true, it was difficult to get into her apartment and it was impossible to think of anyone capable of being murdered there. The fact still remained that she and the Bauers lived their lives in a way for which nothing in a policeman's training prepared him.

The support which she and Emanuel had found in each other in the year following their meeting grew from a relationship for which the English language itself lacked a defining word. Not a friendship, because they were man and woman, not a love affair, because theirs was far more a meeting of minds than of passions, their relationship (an inexact and lifeless term) had given each a vantage point from which to view his life, had given them for a time the gift of laughter and intense discussion whose confidence would be held forever inviolable. They had been lovers for a time—they had no one but themselves to consider—yet this had been far from central to their mutual need. After that first year, they would no more have considered making love than of opening a mink ranch together, yet were there more than a handful of people in the world who could have understood this?

When she reached Nicola's room, Kate, physically exhausted and proportionately less perturbed, found that Nicola's thoughts had been running along the same lines. She had been thinking, that is, not about Emanuel and Kate, but of how few people there were who understood morality apart from convention.

"We have spent this morning and the greater part of yesterday with the police," Nicola said, "being questioned separately, and a bit together, and though they are not actually offensive, as a Berlitz teacher will not actually speak English in teaching you French, they indicate in a thousand little ways that we are both liars, or at least one of us is, and if we would just break down and admit it we would be saving the state and them endless amounts of trouble. Of course, Emanuel has gone stubborn, and won't tell them anything about Janet Harrison. He claims he's not just being noble, guarding the secrets of the confessional and all that; he simply doesn't see what good it would do, for it would probably just get us in deeper. Don't *you* know anything devastating about her, from that college of yours? Why, by the way, aren't you there? It's Friday, isn't it?" Nicola's ability to remember the details of everyone's schedule ("I called because I knew you'd just have gotten in from walking the dog," she had said once to an astonished and recent acquaintance) was one of the most notable things about her.

"I got someone else to take my classes," Kate said. "I didn't feel up to it." She was, in fact, extremely guilty about this, remembering someone's definition of the professional as the man who could perform even when he didn't feel like it.

"The horrible thing is," Nicola continued, "none of them understands in the least what we're like; they all think we're some special species of madmen who have taken to psychiatry because all sane pursuits are beyond us. I don't mean that they don't know all about psychiatry in a theoretical sort of way—I suppose they are used to the testimony of psychiatrists and all that—but people like us who take unscheduled walks, and talk frankly about jealousy and feelings of aggression, and yet insist that because we talk about them we are not likely to act them out, well, the only thing about me that seemed to make sense to one detective was that my father had gone to Yale Law School. They got out of me that you and Emanuel had once been lovers, by the way, and then concluded, I am certain, that we must all be living in some fantastic Noel Cowardish sort of way because we are all friends now and I allow you into my house. You know, Kate, they could understand a man's cheating on his expense account, or going out with call girls when his wife thinks he's on a business trip, but I think we frighten them because we claim to be honest underneath, though a bit casual on the surface, whereas they understand dishonesty, but not the abandonment of surface rectitude. Probably they are convinced there's something indecent about a man's taking twenty dollars from a woman so that she can lie on a couch and talk to him."

"I think," Kate said, "that the police are rather like the English as Mrs. Patrick Campbell saw them. She said the English didn't care what people did as long as they didn't do it in the street and frighten the horses. I don't suppose the police are actively opposed to anything about Emanuel or you or me or psychiatry. It's just that all this has frightened the horses, and unfortunately the police do not sufficiently understand the integrity of psychiatry —where it is practiced with integrity, and we might as well admit it isn't always—to know that Emanuel is the last person who could have murdered the girl. Where *were* you, yesterday morning, by the way, and why the hell didn't you mention that you hadn't been to your analyst's when you were outlining the day?"

"How did you learn I hadn't been there?"

"I have my methods; answer the questions."

"I don't know why I didn't tell you, Kate. I meant to, every time it came up, but one dislikes behaving like a coward, and dislikes even more talking about it. Believe it or not—and the police don't—I was walking around in the park, by the castle and the lake there, where the Japanese cherry blossoms are. It's always been my favorite place, ever since I was very little and held my breath and turned blue if the nurse tried to go somewhere else."

"But *why, why* did you have to pick this one morning to revive childhood memories, when you could have been doing it on Dr. Sanders' couch, and giving yourself a magnificent alibi at the same time?"

"Nobody told me Janet Harrison was going to be murdered on Emanuel's couch. At any rate, I think it's better this way; if I had an alibi, that would leave Emanuel the chief and only suspect. This way, the police aren't quite ready to arrest him. After all, they've got just as much against me as against Emanuel."

"Does the psychiatrist's wife usually come in, in a natural sort of way, and sit down behind the patient? Never mind; I still want to know why you didn't go to your appointment with Dr. Sanders."

"Kate, you're getting like the police, wanting neat,

reasonable answers to everything. There are some people who keep every appointment with their analyst, and always arrive promptly—I'm sure there are—but more people like me turn cowardly. There are several common defenses: arriving late, saying nothing, talking about other matters and avoiding the troublesome problem—in which case, of course, one just keeps coming back to it until one does face it. Mostly I use the system of intellectualizing, but on *the* day I just felt it was spring and I couldn't manage it. I got as far as Madison Avenue and decided, so I went to the park instead. Needless to say, I had no idea Emanuel would be wandering around the park at the same time."

"Did you call Dr. Sanders and say you weren't coming?"

"Of course; it would be most unfair to keep him sitting there, instead of letting him have the hour free. Possibly *he* likes to run around the reservoir; it's a pity he didn't; he might have met Emanuel."

"Would Emanuel know him?"

"Well, they're both at the institute."

"Nicki, did anybody see you leave for what you thought would be an appointment with your psychiatrist? Did anyone see you make the telephone call at Madison Avenue?"

"No one saw me make the phone call. But Dr. Barrister saw me leave. Almost always he's busy with patients at that time, but today, for some reason, he was at the door, showing a patient out or something. *He* saw me leave, but what does that prove? I could easily have come back and stabbed the girl."

"What sort of doctor is he?"

"Woman. I mean, he treats women."

"Gynecology? Obstetrics?"

"No, he doesn't seem to operate very much, and he certainly doesn't do obstetrics; he doesn't strike me as the sort who would want to be dragged out of the theater or out of bed to deliver babies. Emanuel looked him up, actually, on my insistence, and he's got excellent credentials. Emanuel doesn't like him."

"Why not?"

"Well, partly because Emanuel doesn't *like* most people, particularly not people who are smooth, but mostly, I gather, because Barrister and he met once in the hall, and Barrister mentioned something to the effect that they were both doing the same sort of work, and at least neither of them ever buried any patients. A turn, I guess, on the old joke about the dermatologist who never cures anyone and never kills anyone, but it annoyed Emanuel, who said Barrister sounded like a doctor in the movies."

"Well, nature does imitate art; Oscar Wilde was quite right."

"I told Emanuel it was plain envy. Dr. Barrister is very good-looking."

"He sounds more suspicious by the minute; I just about decided, the other night, that he must have done it."

"I know. I've been searching madly for suspects myself and one of the problems is that we aren't exactly seething with suspects. Apart from you and me, and Emanuel, who are innocent by definition, so to speak, we have only the elevator man, Dr. Barrister or his patients or nurse, the patients on either side of Janet Harrison or the homicidal maniac. Not very encouraging. Actually, this whole thing is horrible for Dr. Barrister, though he's been quite nice about it. Police questioning him, and a policeman in the hall outside his office—his patients may not care for that—and then being dragged in by me to look at a body. The fact is, if he were going to murder someone he'd want to murder her as far from himself as possible."

"We've left out one other possible suspect: someone Janet Harrison met here by arrangement. He canceled the patients, saw that everyone had left, enticed her into the office and killed her."

"Kate, you're a genius! That's exactly how it must have happened."

"No doubt. All we've got to do is find this man, *if* he exists."

It was, however, with this probably nonexistent man in mind, that Kate tracked Emanuel down in his office some time later. She had, of course, determined that he was free, and, knocking first, had gone in and shut the door behind her.

"Emanuel, I am sorry, or have I said that already? I keep thinking of all this as like Greek drama; that from the moment of that collision off the Merritt Parkway, we have been heading for this crisis. I suppose there is

51

some comfort in thinking, however literarily, that fate concerns itself with our destinies."

"I've thought much the same thing myself; you weren't sure you wanted to be a college teacher, and I had all sorts of ambivalences about psychiatry. Yet here we are, you as a teacher having sent me, a psychiatrist, one of your students as a patient. It seems to have a pattern, yet of course it can't. If we could just show that it hasn't a pattern, or that we're seeing the pattern the wrong way, we'd be clear of all this."

"Emanuel! I think you've just said something very important and profound."

"Have I? It doesn't seem to make any sense at all."

"Well, never mind; I'm sure the reason for its profundity will occur to me later. What I want now is to have you sit down at your desk and tell me everything you know about Janet Harrison. Perhaps what you say will remind me of something I know, and have forgotten. I'm convinced of one thing: if we find the murderer, always supposing he isn't a homicidal maniac casually in off the streets, we will find him through some knowledge we get about that girl. Will you try to be helpful?"

Rather to Kate's surprise he didn't flatly refuse, he merely shrugged, and continued to gaze out of the window onto a courtyard in which there was almost certainly nothing to see. Kate, with a certain studied carelessness, sat down on the couch. One of the chairs would have been more comfortable, but not to sit on the couch was to avoid it.

"What can I tell you? The tape recording of an analysis, for example, would be meaningless, in any important sense, to someone not trained to interpret. It's not full of clues like a Sherlock Holmes detective story, at least not the sort of clues that would be any use to a policeman. She didn't tell me one day that she would probably be murdered, and that if she were, such-and-such a person would probably have done it. Believe me, had she said something definite of that sort, I would not hesitate to reveal it, certainly not from any misguided sense of idealism. The other vital thing to remember is that, to the analyst, it is unimportant whether something actually happened, or whether the occurrence was merely a fantasy on the part of the patient. To the analyst, there is no essential difference; to the policeman there is, of course, all the difference in the world."

"I should think it would matter very much to a patient whether something had really happened or not. I should think that would be the whole point."

"Exactly. But you would be wrong. And I can't explain all this simply, without grossly falsifying it, and by making it too simple, making it false. But if you want, I'll give you, reluctantly, an example. When Freud began on his treatment of patients, he was astonished to discover how many women in Vienna had had, as children, sexual relations with their fathers. It appeared for a time that at least a handful of Viennese fathers had been sexual maniacs. Then Freud realized that none of these sexual experiences had ever taken place, that they had been fantasies. But his important realization came with the understanding that, for the purposes of the patients' psychological development (though not of course for the purposes of sexual morality in Vienna) it did not matter at all whether the incidents had taken place actually or not. The fantasy had an immense importance of its own. Kate, have you ever tried to explain *Ulysses* to a self-satisfied person whose idea of a great novelist was Lloyd Douglas?"

"All right, all right, I see your point, really I do. But let me go on being a nuisance, will you? I never knew, for example, why she thought she needed an analyst. What did she say the first time she came to see you?"

"The beginning is always rather routine. I ask, of course, what the trouble is. Her answer was not unusual. She slept badly, had a work problem, was unable to read for more than a short period, and had difficulty, as she put it in regrettable social-worker jargon, in relating to people. Her use of that term was the most significant thing she said that day; it indicated how the problem was intellectualized, to what degree emotion had unconsciously been withdrawn from it. Most of this policemen could discover; the rest they would find useless to their purpose. I asked her to tell me something about herself; that's routine also. The facts are usually not important, but the omissions may be greatly so. She was the only child of strict, compulsive parents, both now dead. They were quite old when she was born—if you want the details

I can look them up. She neglected to mention at that time any love affairs, even of the most casual nature, though it emerged later that she had had one love affair in which she was deeply involved. Occasionally associations would bring her to this, break through her resistance, but she always immediately moved away from the subject. We had just begun to touch on some real material when this happened."

"Emanuel, don't you see how important that is? By the way, had she—was she a virgin?" He turned to her with surprise, at the question, at Kate's asking it. Kate shrugged. "Possibly my salacious mind, but I have an odd feeling it may be important."

"I don't know the answer, as a fact, for certain. If you want my professional guess, I would say that the love affair had been consummated. But it's a guess."

"Do patients in the beginning talk mostly about the past or present?"

"About the present; the past of course comes in, more and more as you continue. I had a hunch—though do try not to overestimate its importance—that there was something in the present she was *not* mentioning, something connected, though perhaps only in the sense of the same guilt, with the love affair. Ah, I particularly admire you when you get that gleam in your eye like a hawk about to dive. Do you think she was a key figure in a drug ring?"

"You can laugh later; one other question. You mentioned the other evening that she had become angry, that transference had begun. What is transference when it's at home, as Molly Bloom would say?"

"I loathe simplified explanations of psychiatry. Let's say merely that the anger inherent in some situation becomes directed at the analyst, who becomes the object of those emotions."

"Don't you see, Emanuel? That's good enough. Put together two things you've casually told me. One, possibly connected with her past, which she was hiding. Two, emotion had begun to be generated in her relationship with you. Conclusion: she might have told you, or might have revealed to your sensitive professional ear something which someone didn't want anyone to know. Perhaps there was someone to whom she talked—*she* thought casually

—about her analysis—people do talk *somewhat* about their analyses; I know, I've heard them—and whoever that person was knew she had to die. It was easy enough to discover from her the routine around here, and he came in and killed her, leaving you with the body. Q.E.D."

"Kate, Kate, I have never heard such drastic oversimplification."

"Nonsense, Emanuel. What you lack, what all psychiatrists lack, if you'll forgive my saying so, is a firm grip on the obvious. Well, I won't keep you. But promise me, at any rate, that you'll answer any idiotic questions that I want to ask."

"I promise to cooperate in your gallant attempt to save me from disaster. But you know, my dear, speaking of the obvious, the police have quite a case."

"They don't know you; that's the advantage I have over them. They don't know the sort you are."

"Or the sort Nicola is?"

"No," Kate said. "Not that either. It'll come out all right; you'll see."

She felt, nonetheless, as she stood indecisively in the hall, like a knight who has set off to slay the dragon but has neglected to ask in what part of the world the dragon may be found. It was all very well to decide upon action, but what action, after all, was she to take? As was her habit, she extracted notebook and pen and began to make a list: see Janet Harrison's room, and talk to people who knew her in dormitory; find out about ten and twelve o'clock patients; find out who person in picture Janet Harrison had was (lists always had a devastating effect on Kate's syntax).

"I'm sorry to intrude. Is Mrs. Bauer in?" Kate, who had been writing with the notebook balanced against her purse, dropped notebook, pen and purse. The man stooped with her to help her retrieve the articles, and as they straightened up Kate became aware of that peculiar quality of masculine beauty to which no woman can help reacting, however superficially. It did not really attract Kate, yet she felt herself become somehow more girlish in its presence. She remembered once having met at a dinner party a beautiful, modest young Swedish man. He had perfect manners, there was not anything even suggestive of flirtation in his manner, yet Kate had been horrified to notice that every woman in the room seemed aware of him; her horror had turned to amusement as later, when he had spoken to her, she had found herself simpering.

This man was not that young; his hair was flecked with gray at the temples. "You're Dr. Barrister, aren't you?" Kate said. With difficulty she kept herself from adding, "our favorite suspect." "I'm Kate Fansler, a friend of Mrs. Bauer's; I'll call her."

As Kate walked to the back of the apartment for Nicola, she realized how great, in fact, was the connection between appearance and reality. Considered in the abstract, good looks seemed sinister; yet, in the presence of good looks, Kate found them innocent. It was, of course, no accident that in Western literature, certainly in Western folklore, beauty and innocence were usually joined.

The three of them ended by standing, on this patient-less day, in the living room. Not that Nicola had asked them to sit down; it was not so much that Nicola ignored the social amenities—she seemed never to have known that they existed.

"I stopped in to see how you were bearing up," Dr. Barrister said to Nicola. "I know there's nothing I can do, but I find it difficult to resist the impulse to be neighborly, even in New York where neighbors are not supposed to know one another."

"Aren't you from New York?" Kate asked, to say something.

"Are any New Yorkers?" he asked.

"I am," said Nicola, "and my father before me. *His* father, however, came from Cincinnati. Where are you from?"

"One of those highbrow critics has discovered, I understand, a new sort of novel about the young man from the provinces. I was a young man from the provinces. But you haven't told me how it's all going."

"Emanuel has had to call off the patients for today. We hope in a day or two he can get back to having patients."

"I hope so too. Do let me know, won't you, if there's anything I can do? I'm full of good will, but rather lacking in ideas."

"I know," Nicola said. "For a death in the family or

56

illness, one sends flowers or food. In this case I suppose all you can do is to keep telling everyone that Emanuel and I didn't do it. Kate is full of ideas and is going to find the murderer." Dr. Barrister looked at Kate with interest.

"Where I'm going," said Kate, "is home."

"I'm going east," Dr. Barrister said. "Can I drop you anywhere?"

"That's very kind of you," Kate said, "but I'm going west."

It was as Kate was sitting in the taxi going home that she thought of Jerry.

chapter 6

IT WAS true, of course, that Kate still had the weekend, before Monday should again bring the need to teach her classes. But some preparation for those classes was necessary, particularly since, in the last two days, she had got completely out of touch with the academic world, as though she had been absent for a year. One had, after all, a commitment to one's profession, in spite of any murders, however demanding of investigation.

And what, when she came right down to it, was she to investigate? Something, certainly, could be gleaned by a little recondite questioning around the dormitory where Janet Harrison had lived; examination of the university records might reveal some clue of interest. All that Kate could, without undue interference with her professional duties, undertake. But the police had more or less covered the ground, and what seemed now most fruitful of examination was the other suspects whom the police seemed inclined to treat with little more than superficial interest: the patients before and after Janet Harrison, both men; the elevator man; and any stray men who might, hopefully, turn up and turn out to have known Janet Harrison, however slightly.

It seemed to Kate that, the question of time apart, what was clearly needed was a male investigator, preferably unattached and footloose, able to appear either the worldly young college graduate, possessed of that patina which only the more elegant colleges provide, or the young workingman, who has labored by day and who, in the proper clothes, can hang around discussing ball clubs and whatever else workingmen discuss, without appearing to be slumming. The description fit Jerry to a fare-thee-well, and indicated, once again, the occasional benefits of a large family.

Not that Jerry was in any way related to Kate; not, that is, as yet. But he would one day soon be a nephew by marriage. Kate did not remember his exact age, but he was old enough to vote and young enough to believe that life still held infinite possibilities. "No young man thinks that he shall ever die." Hazlitt had certainly described Jerry.

Kate, coming from a large family, had also been an only child, a unique combination of benefits. Her parents, in the normal course of events—in the normal course, that is, of a sophisticated, well-to-do, New York City life (with summers in Nantucket)—had produced three sons in the first eight years of their marriage. They had departed from convention, or perhaps from what Kate had come to think of as a planned economy, only far enough to find themselves, when the youngest of their sons was fourteen, with an infant daughter. They had provided Kate with a nurse, and subsequently, a governess, loved her to distraction, indulged her recklessly, and stood by hopelessly as she turned her back on society and became, not only an "intellectual," but a Ph.D. This was blamed, somewhat unfairly, on the fact that she had been named Kate, because all her mother remembered of college English was that this had been Shakespeare's favorite female name. The brothers had all pursued more respected and orderly careers. Sarah Fansler, the daughter of the oldest brother, was engaged to Jerry.

Jerry, of course, was moderately unsuitable. Had he been magnificently unsuitable, say a garage mechanic, the engagement would probably at any cost have been stopped. But to have absolutely put the family foot down on Jerry would have been to have turned one's back—the family was very given to bodily metaphors, usually mixed—on the American dream. Jerry's father was dead; his mother managed a small gift shop in New Jersey, and had, by devotion and hard work, sent her son through college; she would also help to send Jerry through law school beginning next fall. Jerry had won scholarships, had worked summers and after school, had helped in the gift shop, and had an air of understanding the world and conjuring it into releasing its gifts. Jerry, just finished with his six months in the Army, was driving a truck for a frozen-foods distributor until the fall. Kate thought he might be willing to do something a bit more adventurous for an equal amount of money.

A call to Jerry at his mother's home in Jersey found him just returned from work, and quite willing (rather to Kate's surprise) to drive in that very evening and talk to her; it appeared that a friend's car was available. Kate managed to suggest that he keep his destination, and the phone call, secret, without sounding, she hoped, as conspiratorial as she felt. It was odd, she realized, that she should be prepared to trust in this way a young man she had met only a few times at those family celebrations of the engagement she had consented to attend. They had been attracted to each other by the amused air of detachment which, alone of those present, they had both radiated. What are *we* doing here? they seemed, smilingly, to ask each other. Kate was there because she admitted some, though not many, family obligations, and Jerry was there because Sarah was very pretty and very proper. Kate had always thought her rather dull, but Jerry was, perhaps, just smart enough in the ways of the world to prefer a dull, conventional, though pretty, wife.

When he arrived, Kate offered him a beer and plunged right into the matter at hand: "I'm going to offer you a job," she said. "The same pay as you're getting now. Can you take a leave, and go back when you want to?"

"Probably. But I get time and a half on this job for working extra hours." He was relaxed, prepared to be enlightened and, Kate suspected, entertained.

"I'll pay you only the regular amount. This job will be much more interesting, and require more of your talents. But if you succeed, I'll give you a bonus at the end."

"What's the job?"

"Before I tell you that, I want a solemn promise of secrecy. No one is to be told about this—not your family, or your friends; not by the slightest hint are they to know what you're involved in. Not even Sarah is to suspect."

"Agreed. Like Hamlet's friends, I won't even indicate that I might tell if I would. I swear on the sword. Very good play, I thought," he added, before Kate could control her look of surprise. "I promise not to murmur a word to Sarah." It seemed to Kate that his willingness to keep things from Sarah did not bode well for their marriage, but she was past having scruples about any good fortune that came her way.

"Very well, then. I want you to help me solve a murder. No, I have not taken leave of my senses, nor have I developed paranoia or megalomania. Have you read anything about this girl who was murdered on the psychoanalyst's couch? You could scarcely have helped it, I suppose. They think the psychoanalyst did it; he's a very good friend of mine, and I want to prove that he didn't do it, nor did his wife, who is the suspect they're holding in abeyance. But I'm convinced the only way to prove Emanuel didn't do it is to find out who did. A young man like you can talk naturally to a lot of people, can ask questions I can't ask. Also, by the end of spring term the work at college reaches monumental proportions. Get the picture?"

"What about the police?"

"The police are very conscientious, in their unimaginative way. Perhaps I'm prejudiced; probably I am. But they have such a nice suspect, they are so certain that no one else *could* have done it, that their searches in other directions are bound to be somewhat lacking in vigor, or so it seems to me. However, if we find a nice fat clue leading to someone else, I imagine they can be persuaded to follow it up."

"Have *you* a favorite suspect?"

"Unfortunately, no. We're not only lacking in suspects; we're delightfully free of information of any kind."

"Perhaps the girl was drugged. Then anyone could have put her on the couch and murdered her, having got rid of the analyst first."

"You sound very promising. As a matter of fact, though, we do have some information about the murder, if not about other suspects or the girl. She wasn't drugged. If you want the job, I'll tell you all about it. It won't take long."

It took, however, longer than Kate would have thought. She told Jerry the whole thing from the beginning, starting with her recommendation of the girl to Emanuel. He listened closely, and asked a number of intelligent questions. Kate realized that she was offering him adventure with the pay of security, and it might well warp his whole view of life. The younger generation, so all the

61

journalists said—and it was generally true enough to be frightening—opted always for security, for the sure job, the sure pension, the sure way of life. They might have liked adventure, but they didn't want to pay the price for it; better to read *Kon-Tiki* in an air-conditioned study in Westchester. Jerry was getting adventure, and a salary check determined by a union. It might not be the best training for a young man, but when you came right down to it, finding bodies on the couch was not the best training for a psychoanalyst either.

In any case, there was nothing for Jerry to do until Monday. He promised to come for orders then, late afternoon, by which time he hoped to have disentangled himself from frozen food, and thought up a plausible story, should one be required. Jerry's departure was speeded by a telephone. The call was from Reed. No, he had no other news, but he did have a copy of the picture. Two copies? Yes, she could have two copies. He would bring them up tonight, if that was all right. How about a movie to get their minds off things? Danny Kaye? Heartlessly, Kate agreed.

After the movie, Reed and Kate went out for a meal. Kate took from her purse the picture of the young man. She had looked at the face so steadily that it seemed almost as though the picture might be induced to speak. "The question is," Kate said, "is this the young man of the love affair?" She told Reed about her conversation with Emanuel. "How old would you say this young man is?" Kate asked.

"Perhaps thirty, perhaps twenty-five. He looks very young; at the same time he looks like someone who looks young for his age, if you follow me."

"I follow you. He keeps reminding me of someone."

"Probably of himself; you keep staring at the picture."

"No doubt you are right." Kate put the young man firmly away.

"A conscientious young detective trotted all over the dormitory with that picture," Reed said. "He is a very attractive young man, and the girls and women were delighted to chat with him about anything. They would gladly have said they saw this young man of the picture every day of their lives, to make the detective happy, but the truth was no one had ever laid eyes on him. One older woman thought she recognized him, but it turned out she was thinking of Cary Grant in his younger days. If that young man, or his picture, has ever been around that dormitory, he managed to avoid being seen by anyone, including, incidentally, the service people, who were also questioned. Kate, you realize he is probably a perfectly ordinary young man who jilted her, or, to be less cynical, got himself killed in a war or an accident, leaving her forever bereft."

"He's not as good-looking as Cary Grant. He doesn't look movie-actorish at all."

"Kate, you're beginning to worry me. Are you . . . does this man, this Emanuel Bauer mean so much to you?"

"Reed, if I can't make you understand this, how are the police ever to understand Emanuel? He's the last married man in the world likely to become involved with a woman, let alone a patient. But even if all that were possible, which I don't for a minute grant, don't you see that his office, his couch—these are the setting of his profession? Can't you see that no genuine psychoanalyst with Emanuel's training would be overcome by maniacal passion in his office hours? Even admitting (which I do not) that he might commit any crime as a man, he could not commit one as a psychiatrist."

"Have psychiatrists so much more integrity than other people?"

"No, of course not. Many psychiatrists I know of are the scum of the earth. They discuss their patients at parties. They grow rich, and brag about the fees they charge; they are paid $150 for their signature on a piece of paper releasing a patient from some institution. The signature means that the patient will be under their care, but they sign and are paid, and hear no more of it. Even one signature a day is a nice yearly income. There are psychiatrists who entertain doctors, so that the doctors will refer patients to them. All charged up to the expense account, of course. But Emanuel, and others like him, love their work; and if you want my recipe for integrity, find the man who loves his work and loves the cause he serves by doing it. How's that for pomposity?"

"What is the cause? Helping people?"

"Oddly enough, no. I don't think so—not for Emanuel

at any rate. He is interested in discovering something about the workings of the human mind. If you were to ask him, he would probably say that analysis is most important for research, that therapy is more or less a by-product. What would the D.A.'s office make of that?"

"Kate, forgive me, but you were lovers; that came out in the testimony of the wife, though she did not in any sense offer it. I think the detectives were looking around generally for motives."

"Then Nicola should have murdered me, or I should have murdered Nicola. Except that we all understand it was a long, long time ago, and never were any embers colder."

"Where did you and Emanuel meet, back in the days when the embers weren't so cold?"

"I had an apartment back in those days, too. Are you trying to make me out a scarlet woman? Reed, why do I keep forgetting you're a policeman?"

"Because I'm not a policeman. At the moment, I'm the lawyer for the prosecution. Did Emanuel have an office in those days?"

"He shared a little office with another analyst."

"Did you ever meet him there?"

"Yes, I guess so, once or twice."

"Were you ever—together—on the couch?"

"Reed, I've underestimated you. You'll make an excellent, quite diabolic prosecutor, able not only to elicit half-guessed-at facts, but able also to distort them and avoid the truth. On the witness stand, of course, I wouldn't be able to explain. The truth, nonetheless, is that Emanuel had just begun in those days. He was doing therapy, so he didn't use the couch, which happened to be part of the furniture—for future use, perhaps. And I was never there in office hours."

"Kate, my dear, I'm trying to show you what you're up against, plunging into this thing without any idea of what you're getting into. I know, fools rush in where angels fear to tread; but I've never discovered what, if anything, the fools accomplished. No, I'm not calling you a fool. I'm trying to say that you've set out, gallantly, God knows, to save Emanuel, and you may end up only muddying the waters and ruining yourself. And if there is no longer anything between you, as they say in

64

the worst sort of magazines, why are you doing it? From a disinterested love of truth?"

"I'm not ready to admit that that's the worst motive in the world. I'm too old to be newly shocked by the fact that everyone can be bought, that corruption is the only way of existence; every graduation speech, and I have heard many, moans on about corruption. The only thing I know is that here and there one finds someone interested in truth, in goodness, if you insist, for its own sake. How many policemen are there in New York who have never received a dollar outside their salary? All right, perhaps I'm rambling. Look at it in the cold-blooded way you prefer. Emanuel had four years of college, four years' of medical school, one year's general internship, two years' residence in psychiatry, three years' training at the institute, and many, many valuable years of experience. Is all this to go down the drain because some clever murderer killed a girl in his office?"

"I was always under the impression that you had relatively little faith in psychiatry."

"As a therapeutic tool it is, I think, very clumsy, to say the best that can be said about it. I have many other objections to it. But what has that to do with seeing an able psychiatrist condemned for something he didn't do? There are many things I don't admire about Emanuel, but I feel about him as Emerson felt about Carlyle: 'If genius were cheap,' Emerson said, 'we might do without Carlyle, but in the existing population he cannot be spared.' "

"May I ask where you intend to begin?"

"It would be less embarrassing if you didn't. Have you found out anything about the other patients?"

"The ten o'clock patient is named Richard Horan. Twenty-eight, unmarried, works for an advertising firm. Was planning to switch his hour as soon as possible, since it was convenient neither for him nor Emanuel, though I gather, *entre nous*, that advertising firms are used to having their personnel in analysis. We live in a fascinating time; there's no getting away from that. The twelve o'clock patient teaches English, I'm sure you'll be delighted to hear, at one of the city colleges. I can't remember which one, but a long subway ride is involved. Also unmarried, and not likely to marry, if the impression of the detective is worth anything; it may not be. Your Eman-

65

uel, as usual, is mum, though here I rather respect his point of view. Obviously he can't talk about the patients who haven't been murdered. This patient's name is Frederick Sparks, as you know, but I'll send you a copy of the notes; you will then be in a position to blackmail *me*. Do I make my trust and confidence clear?"

"Can I have their home addresses?"

"You can have anything it is in my power to give you. Just let me know what you're doing, will you, in a general sort of way? And if you get a note to meet a mysterious man with interesting information on some dark street, don't go."

"Flippancy," Kate said flippantly, "will get you nowhere. May I have another cup of coffee?"

chapter 7

BY MONDAY morning life had become, not normal certainly, but with the appearance of being normal. Emanuel returned—minus his eleven o'clock patient—to the practice of psychiatry. Nicola attended her own psychoanalytic hour. Kate, who had disciplined herself to the preparation of work over the weekend, returned to teaching. Saturday evening she had spent with a painter who read only French newspapers, was interested in murder, and had theories about nothing but art. This helped considerably.

But the chief factor in removing the Bauers from the center of attention and the glare of publicity was a horrible crime in Chelsea: some madman had enticed away, raped and murdered a four-year-old girl. The police and newspapers, for the time being at least, switched their main forces elsewhere. (The madman was captured, quite easily, a week later, which brought some comfort to Kate. Madmen, she reasoned, were usually caught. Therefore Janet Harrison could not have been killed by a madman. She found this magnificent piece of illogic quite consoling.)

At ten o'clock on Monday morning Kate lectured on *Middlemarch*. Did anything, after all, matter beside the fact that imagination might create worlds like *Middlemarch*, that one might learn to perceive these worlds and the structures that sustained them? Looking through the novel the night before, Kate had come upon a sentence which seemed oddly applicable: "Strange that some of us, with quick alternate vision, see beyond our infatuations, and even while we rave on the heights, behold the wide plain where our persistent self pauses and awaits us." Really, the sentence had nothing to do with the present case: a murder was not an infatuation. Yet, after the lecture,

Kate realized that while she had discussed *Middlemarch,* she had been incapable of thinking of anything else. The persistent self lived, she thought, in that work where one's attention was wholly caught. Emanuel, listening behind the couch, knew perhaps the same thing. It occurred to Kate that few people possessed "persistent selves," and that Emanuel, as one of them, had to be saved.

She therefore turned her steps, after the lecture, to the Graduate Women's Dormitory, where Janet Harrison had lived. Not many of the students, as Kate had told Detective Stern, lived on the campus, but the university maintained a dormitory for women who wanted to live, or whose parents insisted that they live, under more proper and controlled circumstances. The dormitory was a benefit also to students who did not want to be burdened with any domestic concerns, and it seemed likely that Janet Harrison had chosen to live there for that reason.

Kate had worked out an extremely complicated plan of attack upon the dormitory, which involved a certain amount of strolling around corridors, conferences with porters and maids, perhaps the exchange of muted confidences with the woman in charge of the dormitory; but the need for all this was obviated by Kate's colliding, on the doorstep, with Miss Lindsay. Last year Miss Lindsay had been a student of Kate's in a course in advanced writing which Kate had taken over for a professor on leave and abandoned upon his return with greater relief than she had ever felt before. The course, nonetheless, had had its moments, and Miss Lindasy, whose main subjects were Latin and Greek, had provided most of them. Kate still cherished, in fact, a Latin translation of "Twinkle, Twinkle, Little Star," beginning *Mica, mica, parva stella, Micor quae nam sis, tam bella,* with which Miss Lindsay had presented her on some now quite forgotten occasion. Kate's own Latin, despite a fascinated reading, some years ago, of Virgil's *Aeneid,* was still of the *hic, haec, hoc* variety.

Miss Lindsay was that rare student who can talk informally with a professor without ever crossing the line into familiarity. She followed Kate now, willingly enough, into the lounge, abandoning her destination without a pang. Kate, who needed her, did not argue very strenuously. It occurred to her, not for the first time, that in the solution of a murder Kant's categorical imperative had continually to be ignored. Kate asked Miss Lindsay if she had known Janet Harrison.

"Slightly," Miss Lindsay said. If she was surprised at the question she did not show it. "We have, of course, been talking of nothing else for days. As a matter of fact, the only time I spoke to her, we spoke of you. You are the only teacher who seemed to arouse her out of her usual academic lassitude. Something to do with moral obligations struck her particularly, as I remember."

"Doesn't she seem to you an odd sort of person to have been murdered? Not, of course, that one exactly expects anyone to be murdered, but she seemed so, I think 'uninvolved' is the word I want, so unlikely, despite her beauty, to inspire passion."

"I don't agree. In the town I came from there was a girl like that, distant, you know, and rather above it all; but it came out finally that she had been living, ever since she was fifteen, with a grocer whom everyone thought to be happily married. Not so much still waters, but calm waters with a lethal current underneath. Of course, I could be quite wrong about Janet Harrison. The person you want to talk to is Jackie Miller. She has a room near Janet's. Jackie is the sort who talks all the time and never seems to listen, yet she punctuates the flow with pointed questions one somehow can't avoid answering. She knows more about everyone than anybody else. Perhaps you know the type?" Kate merely groaned. She knew the type all too well. "Why not come up and see her now? She's probably just getting up, and if you can once start her talking, she'll tell you everything anyone could know. I believe," Miss Lindsay added, leading the way upstairs, "that it was she who told the detective that Janet had always carried a notebook. No one else had noticed."

Jackie responded to their knock by flinging open the door and waving them gleefully into the messiest room Kate had seen since her college days. Jackie, dressed in a sleeping outfit of very short pants and a lacy, sleeveless top that seemed quite wasted in a woman's dormitory, was making herself a cup of instant coffee with water from the tap. She offered them some; Miss Lindsay refused with commendable firmness, but Kate meekly accepted hers in the hope that this would lead them sooner to the point. She might, however, have saved herself from the agony of drinking the concoction.

"So you're Professor Fansler," Jackie began. She was clearly the sort who a hundred years ago would have tossed aside her parasol and said, "So you're President Lincoln." "I keep hearing about you from all the students, but I just can't seem to work one of your courses into my schedule. All my credits from Boston University were in literature—I just love reading novels—so I have to spend all my time here taking courses in other ghastly things. But I must fit in one of your courses because they all say you're one of the few professors who manage to be entertaining and profound; and let's admit it, most women professors are dreadfully dull old maids." It did not apparently occur to Jackie that there was anything infelicitous about this statement. Kate fought down the outrage which such a generalization always aroused in her.

"Janet Harrison was a student of mine," she said, without too much finesse. But finesse would undoubtedly be wasted on Jackie.

"Yes, I know. She mentioned it once at lunch, and usually you know she never so much as uttered—the strong silent type, not at all attractive, I think, in a woman. Anyway, this day at lunch (you must have had your mouth full, Kate thought maliciously) she said that you said that Henry James had said that morality depended— the morality of one's actions, that is—depended, or should depend, on the moral quality of the person who was going to do the action and not on the moral quality of the person one was doing the action to. Of course," Jackie added, with the first sign of insight Kate had seen in her, "she put it better. But the point was, she didn't agree. She thought if someone was morally bad, you should do something about it because of their morality, not because of yours." Kate, gallantly allowing herself and Henry James to be so traduced, wondered if Janet Harrison had indeed said something of the sort. *Could* she have gotten wind of a drug ring?

"Of course," Jackie continued, "she was frigid, poor thing, and completely unable to relate to people. I told her so and she practically admitted it. I guessed, of course, that she was being analyzed. She used to leave here promptly every morning at the same time, and I found out

70

she wasn't going to a class, and a very good thing for her. If you want to know, I think the analyst stabbed her out of sheer frustration. She probably lay there hour after hour not opening her mouth. Have you been analyzed?"

It was nearly a quarter of a century since Kate had felt the impulse to stick out her tongue at someone. "Were any other rooms robbed except hers?" she asked.

"No, it was really very peculiar. I told her she had probably aroused some sort of fetishism in some poor frustrated man. If you ask me, he took the camera as a cover, but he was really looking for something personal; but there really wasn't anything in her room worth looking for"—Jackie slid rather hastily over the unfortunate implications of this remark—"and, of course, she dressed like the matron of a girls' school. I used to tell her she was really very good-looking, if she would only cut her hair instead of just wearing it pulled back, and you know—showed herself off a little. I was fascinated by that picture the detective was showing around here, apparently of someone connected with Janet. Perhaps she did go out to meet a man, after all, though it seems unlikely. If so, she certainly kept him well hidden."

"Did she go out often?"

"Well, not often, but fairly regularly. She went out to dinner, or she would just disappear, and obviously she wasn't going to the library. I think someone saw her with a man once."

"Who?" Kate asked. "Was it someone who saw the picture?"

"The detective asked me that," Jackie said in her maddening way, "and, you know, I can't remember. It was someone I was talking to by the fountain, because I remember that someone had put soap in the fountain, and this girl and I were commenting on that; but I can't remember how the question came up—something like my saying one doesn't expect to find soap in a fountain, and she said, speaking of the unexpected, etcetera. But, you know, I just can't remember who it was. Perhaps I dreamed it all. Of course, she—Janet, I mean—was an only child, and I always think that the reciprocal rivalry of the sibling relationship does a great deal to develop the personality, don't you?"

It was likely that she did not expect an answer, but

71

Kate rose to her feet, with a frank look at her watch. Even for the solution of a murder, there was a point beyond which she would not go. Miss Lindsay joined her in a movement toward the door. "You will let me know, won't you," Kate said, striving for a casual tone, "if you remember who the person was who saw Janet and the man?"

"Why are you so interested?" Jackie asked.

"Thank you for the coffee," Kate flung back, and, closing the door, sped down the corridor with Miss Lindsay.

"It's a pity no one murdered *her*," said Miss Lindsay, echoing Kate's thoughts. "I think even the police would gladly leave it as one of the unsolved cases."

With an intense feeling of frustration, Kate made her way to the office of university records. Here, with a certain amount of what Jerry would probably have called "throwing her weight around," she managed to obtain Janet Harrison's records. For the first and undoubtedly the last time in her life, Kate was grateful to the modern mania for forms. She began with Janet's record at the university; her marks had been B minuses, with an occasional B. To Kate's professional eye, this indicated that her instructors had found her clearly capable of A work, but performing, probably, on the C level. There was a strong tendency among professors, including herself, to save C's for the strictly C students, of whom, God knows, there were enough.

Janet Harrison's college credits were all in order; she had majored in history, with a minor in economics. Then why had she chosen to come to graduate school to study English literature? Well, the fields were not, of course, precisely unrelated. She had apparently applied for, and received, several college loans, and she had also applied for a fellowship. For the details of this application one had to consult the fellowship office.

Cursing, Kate went to consult the fellowship office. Janet had probably gotten the fellowship, but it would be interesting to know. Her marks in college had been almost all A's, though the college, supposedly near her home (Kate was somewhat shaky on the geography of the Midwest) had been too undistinguished to have Phi Beta Kappa. Yet why had a girl who had got A's in her college,

72

however small, fallen to the B-minus level in graduate school? It was almost always the other way around. Probably she had had something else on her mind. In fact, everyone seemed impressed with the fact—now that Kate thought of it—that Janet Harrison had had something on her mind. But what? What?

The fellowship forms were even more demanding than the university forms has been. Where, the fellowship forms wanted to know, had she spent every year of her life? (Leave no gaps! the form stated sternly.) After college, Janet Harrison had gone to the nursing school at the University of Michigan. Nursing school! Now that was certainly odd. History, Nursing school, English literature. Well, young American females did have a way, if they were not early married, of searching about for possible professions, but surely this search was a trifle wide in scope. Perhaps her parents had been of the old-fashioned sort who might send a girl to college, but insisted that she be trained to earn a living. To such people, Kate knew, there were only three ways a girl could be trained to earn a living: by becoming a secretary, a nurse, or a schoolteacher.

But Janet Harrison had not persisted with her nursing. Her father had died a year after she began training, and she had gone home to live with her mother. It was apparently at her mother's death that the girl had come to New York to study English literature. But why come to New York? The damned form raised more questions than it answered. According to the financial statement appended, Janet had been left, on the death of her mother, with some income, but not enough to pay the large fees of the university, unless she also took a job, and the university preferred to lend students money rather than have them try to carry jobs and graduate work at the same time. She had, Kate noticed, got the fellowship, which was not very large.

Kate walked back to the office with questions whirling in her mind. Had Janet Harrison left a will, and if so—or if not—who got her money? Was it possibly worth murdering her for? Reed would have to find that out. Perhaps the police, whom Kate had a regrettable habit of forgetting, had already looked into this. It seemed obvious enough. Why had Janet Harrison come to New

York? The University of Michigan had a perfectly good graduate school. Well, perhaps she had wanted to get away from home, but did it have to be so *far* from home? Why had she chosen so varied a program of study? Why, if it came to that, had she never married? Jackie Miller, blast her loquacious imbecility, might think Janet frigid, or "unable to relate to people" (the girl had, of course, used that very phrase to Emanuel); but she was certainly beautiful and had had, so Emanuel thought, a love affair.

At her office Kate found waiting students and, feeling rather like a trapeze artist, plunged once again into academia.

Exhausted, she reached home later in the afternoon to find Jerry camping on the doorstep. He had the gleam in his eye of the prospector who has found gold. She consoled him for his wait with a beer.

"I have been on the job," he said. "I couldn't reach you this morning, after handing in my temporary resignation, and since I assumed my pay started today, I honorably determined to get to work. You had not, however, left any directions, so I decided to mosey around on my own. I couldn't think of anything else to do, so I went over to that dormitory where Janet Harrison had lived."

"Really," Kate said. "I was there myself. Did you meet Jackie Miller too?"

"I was not concerning myself with females; that, obviously, is your department. I went down to the basement and talked to the porter. Naturally, I didn't ask him a lot of questions about Janet Harrison; that is not, in my opinion, the way to elicit information. I was just a nice eager boy who wanted to know how I could get a porter's job at the university, where I wanted to work, because then I wouldn't have to pay for the courses I wanted to take. Employees don't, you know. We mentioned that the Tigers had a good chance for the pennant, we talked about how much money everything costs, and thus, gradually, did I come into possession of the fact that will save Emanuel, if I may call him that."

"For God's sake, stop being dramatic and get to the point."

"The point, my dear Kate, is that the porter's uniform was stolen on the morning that Janet Harrison's room was robbed. The porter was very exercised about the whole

74

thing, because the university is being stubborn about buying him another one; you know the sort of uniform they wear—blue shirt and trousers, with 'Building and Grounds' stitched on the pocket. All right, all right, don't get hysterical. Obviously, you see, a man stole that uniform to get into Janet Harrison's room. A man can't usually go wandering around female dormitories, as I know to my cost, but no one ever notices a porter; he's obviously on his way to fix something, and no one gives him a second glance.

"Now, the beautiful part of all this is that the porter came on duty at noon, when he noticed the uniform had been stolen, and the room wasn't robbed before ten-thirty, because the maid went in then to straighten up. Therefore the uniform was stolen and the room robbed when Emanuel had a beautiful alibi: he was with a patient, and the patient, ladies and gentlemen, was Janet Harrison, who therefore could not have been in the room either. Therefore the room was *not* robbed by Emanuel, and since I don't see why we shouldn't leap to the conclusion that whoever robbed the room murdered the girl, it wasn't Emanuel."

"He could have hired someone, the police will say."

"But we know he didn't, and we will prove it. Furthermore, I couldn't check on any of the others, but I went around to Emanuel's house for another buddy-buddy chat with the employees—the Tigers really have a good chance of winning the pennant this year—and discovered that the elevator man is off on Friday. Dr. Michael Barrister does not hold office hours on Friday, and if you will give me the names of the ten o'clock and twelve o'clock patients, we will discover shortly what they do on Fridays. I'll bet you my salary, double or nothing, that whoever robbed that room murdered the girl. And I don't think whoever it was relegated the task to anyone. My reasons for thinking that are that it would be too damn inconvenient if he, or she, had. Speaking of shes, Mrs. Bauer—may I call her Nicola?—was probably at her analytic hour with an alibi. But of course it was a man who stole the uniform, so that doesn't get us very much further."

"Jerry, you're wonderful."

"I think perhaps after law school I will join the F.B.I.

75

Do they look for murderers, or only Communists and drug dispensers? I'm rather enjoying this."

"We shall have to map out a plan," Kate said, with a certain amount of primness, to control his exuberant spirits.

"That's simple. Tomorrow morning you return to Thomas Carlyle—if that is the man with whom you were carrying on an affair in the stacks—and I will follow the trail of the ten o'clock patient in the advertising business. You see before you a young man burning with the desire to go into the advertising business. Will you have a thinking man's cigarette?"

chapter 8

JERRY arrived at Kate's apartment the next morning at a quarter to nine. They had decided that he would thus arrive each morning for a conference. Kate assumed, though she did not actually ask him, that his mother, friends, and fiancée still imagined him to be driving the truck.

"One thing's been worrying me," Kate said. "Why didn't the man, whoever he was, return the uniform? If he returned it before twelve the porter would never have known it was gone. Why didn't the porter tell the police it had been stolen, by the way?"

"To answer the second question first, the porter didn't tell the police because he doesn't like the police, and they might have 'pulled him in' or thought he was implicated. The theft of the uniform might well make it look like an inside job."

"How easily you slip into the jargon."

"To answer the first question," said Jerry, ignoring this, "he didn't return the uniform because it was risky enough stealing it. Why risk returning it, and double the chance of getting caught? Also, I imagine, it made it much easier for him to get out of the place unnoticed. A man in a porter's uniform isn't really looked at, but a man in a business suit emerging from a women's dormitory might very well be noticed. Easier to use the uniform for a quick getaway, and then drop it down an incinerator someplace."

"What did he do with his own clothes when he put on the uniform?"

"Really, Kate, you don't seem to have much of a flair for this sort of thing, if you don't mind my mentioning it. He put it on over his own clothes, naturally; the porter is, unfortunately, on the large side, so it's no good looking for a tiny murderer. Those uniforms are, of course, handed around, and are not expected to be more than approximate fits."

"Well," Kate said, "I have, for the moment, decided to abandon Thomas Carlyle. Delightful enough man, in his way, but not exactly restful, and dreadfully time-consuming. I had better take on Frederick Sparks. He is, after all, in my field—I know several people in his English Department, and if there is a motive there, I am likelier than you to smell it out. That leaves you with the advertising business. Perhaps, by tonight, we shall, one or the other, have a suspect bulging with motive. We may, of course, find that our investigations take several days. Perhaps we should keep notes, and when we are finished we can write a manual of do-it-yourself detection. Are you actually going to apply for a job?"

"I haven't really decided yet. You know, I think I'll try to work in Dr. Michael Barrister's nurse. I got a glimpse of her yesterday—very young, very attractive, and, I would guess, very eager to talk, if encouraged immediately after work when she has just spent hours listening to the ailments of aging women. We might as well find out all we can about the sinister doctor across the hall."

"You haven't met him yet. When you do, you will discover that he is, unfortunately, not sinister at all. However, we must search out every avenue of possibility, if that is the correct phrase. Don't, by the way, get so involved with the young, attractive nurse that you forget my investigation and your fiancée."

"I only came to work on the case because all detectives have such a fascinating sex life. Have you read Raymond Chandler?"

"I have read Raymond Chandler, and his detective was not engaged to be married."

"Nor did he have a nice safe job driving around the countryside with frozen food. Nor, now I think of it, did he spend six months in the Army as a cook."

"A *cook!* Why on earth?"

"Because I've never cooked a thing in my life, and had a great deal of experience driving trucks. But they didn't have any room in the transport section because it was

78

all full up with cooks. Do not, in any case, worry about my morals, which, to the extent they are not already corrupted, are incorruptible. I knew a guy who got involved with a redhead after he was engaged to a fetching brunette. He met the redhead in a village nightclub where he had a temporary job playing the bass fiddle. The two women, between them, wore him down to such a state that he joined a ship's orchestra, even though he once got seasick on the boat ride to the Statue of Liberty, and was last heard of in ragged clothes, playing the violin under a balcony in Rome, waiting for Tennessee Williams to work him into his latest play."

He departed, having acquired from Kate a copy of the picture found in Janet Harrison's purse, money, and a key to Kate's apartment, should he require to return to home base when she was gone.

About Frederick Sparks, whose appointment came after Janet Harrison's, and who had been present at the finding of the body, Kate was prepared to indulge the profoundest suspicions. For a few minutes after Jerry's departure she considered calling Emanuel to beg a few minutes in which to discuss Mr. Sparks. It might be Emanuel whose whole professional career—indeed, whose life was in danger— but in Kate's eyes his professional stature had not diminished by one millimeter, and she found this extraordinarily encouraging, even though it meant she begged for, rather than demanded, time. Kate felt certain that Emanuel's patients would think of him in the same way. She would wait till she had met Frederick Sparks, or at least had garnered some impressions of him, before attempting to extricate something from Emanuel.

She was interrupted in these ruminations by a telephone call from Reed, who sounded exactly as Jerry had the night before.

"We have finally discovered something," Reed said, "that, I have a hunch, will break the case, one way or another."

"I know all about the uniform," Kate said primly.

"What uniform?"

"Sorry, I must have been thinking of one of my other cases. What have you found?"

"Janet Harrison left a will."

79

"Did she indeed? I hope she was murdered for her money; what we badly need in this case is a motive."

"She had $25,000 invested in some family business which paid her 6 percent (preferred stock) or, to save you the embarrassment of higher mathematics, $1,500 dollars a year."

"Perhaps the family in the business murdered her for her stock."

"Scarcely. I'm trying to tell you that she left a will. She didn't leave the stock to the family. Who do you think she left it to? Forgive me, whom?"

"If she left it to Emanuel, I shall shoot myself."

"Messy. And people unacquainted with guns usually miss, shatter the walls and frighten the neighbors. She left it to a Daniel Messenger, M.D."

"Who's he? Reed! Could he be the youngish man in the picture?"

"Two minds with but a single thought. Or rather, twenty minds. We have already acquired a description of Dr. Daniel Messenger, who practices medical research—does one practice research? I'm sure not—in Chicago. It's obvious he's older than our man, and couldn't be more unlike the picture if he'd planned it that way, the unspeakable blackguard."

"Perhaps he's disguised—dyed his hair or had plastic surgery."

"Kate, my girl, I get more worried about you every time we have a conversation. We are about to receive a picture of the chap, and I think it will convince even you. I gather no one could mistake him for a young Cary Grant; a young Lon Chaney, in full makeup, would apparently be nearer the mark. His hair grows low on his forehead, he has a long, rather fleshy nose, and his ears stick out. Undoubtedly he has a beautiful personality; he certainly must have character, to go into research, with the money lying around for doctors these days."

"What was he to Janet Harrison, and where did you find the will?"

"What he was to Janet Harrison is the question of the hour. He was interrogated by a Chicago detective who swears that the good doctor had never heard the name, and certainly didn't recognize her picture. There is something about that girl which is beginning to fascinate me.

How we got the will is a demonstration of the benefits of publicity. The lawyer with whom she had left it called us, and turned over the will. No, you need not ask: the lawyer did not know her. She apparently picked his name out of the phone book. He wrote out the will, a perfectly simple one, and charged her fifty dollars. He had been away on some beastly business trip, and the name registered only when his wife talked on about the case after he got home. He seems perfectly genuine. But there *must* be a connection with this Daniel Messenger, though as far as we can figure out he and Janet Harrison have never even been in the same place at the same time."

"Deposit ten cents for the next five minutes, please."

"Reed, you're in a phone booth."

"With practice, my dear, you will make a great detective. I could hardly spill out all these secrets from a phone in the D.A.'s office. Kate, I'm beginning to get interested in your case. This probably proves that insanity is catching. I haven't got a dime." He hung up.

Daniel Messenger. For a few hectic moments Kate toyed with the idea of hopping a plane for Chicago. But, however brutal one might be with Thomas Carlyle, George Eliot had to be coped with tomorrow. And of course, one did not "hop" a plane. One took a long slow ride to an airport, and argued for hours with ticket agents who seemed to have been hired five minutes ago for what they supposed to be another job; and if one survived that, one got to Chicago only to join a "stack" over the airfield there, and then either died of boredom or crashed into a plane that thought it was in the stack over Newark. With an effort, Kate brought her wandering mind back to Frederick Sparks. Reed's call, however, apart from distracting her and thickening the plot, had reminded her of the uses of the telephone. She dialed the number of a professor of sixteenth century literature with whom she had studied for the orals, lo, these many years ago.

"Lillian. This is Kate Fansler."

"Kate! How's everything in the university on the hill?"

"Hideous, as always in the spring." April is the cruelest month. That was how it had begun. For a few moments they chatted about personal things. "I'm calling," Kate continued, "to ask about a colleague of yours. Frederick Sparks."

"If you're thinking of hiring him, don't. In the first place he's got tenure and wouldn't dream of leaving, and in the second place he's a great admirer of closet drama, and thinks *The Cenci* is better than *Macbeth*."

"Nothing was further from my mind than hiring him. I'll tell you another time what this is all about. What's he like?"

"Rather tedious. Good scholar. Lives alone, having recently broken away from mother, at least to that extent. Has a French poodle named Gustave."

"Gustave?"

"After Flaubert. Although his favorite French author is Proust. Gustave's, that is."

"I take it he does not care for women. Sparks, that is."

"Most people take it. Me, I've given up labels. So many incorrect ones have been attached to me that I've abandoned them entirely. Besides, he's being analyzed."

This was a lead which Kate had no wish at the moment to follow. "Lillian, is there some way I could meet Sparks, socially perhaps, or at least casually? Soon, that is."

"You fascinate me. No one's been anxious to meet Sparks since the P. and B. committee considered him for tenure."

"What on earth is the P. and B. committee?"

"Oh, you innocents who do not work for city colleges. No one has the faintest idea what the initials stand for, but it's all-powerful. As a matter of fact, I am going to a party tonight for a colleague who just got a Fulbright to India, and Sparks will undoubtedly be there. I've got a date, but I will drag you along as a cousin of his we couldn't dump. The date's that is. Will that do?"

"That will do gloriously. But the fewer lies, the better, I always think. Let's just say I dropped in on you."

"Very well, you mysterious creature. Drop in on me about eight. Bring a bottle for the festivities, and you will be triply welcomed. See you then."

Which left Kate with nothing to do but get back to work and wonder what Jerry was up to. Richard Horan, of the advertising business, must by now be settled down on Emanuel's couch. Dr. Barrister's pretty nurse must be involved with the women patients. Jerry, for all his detective pose, was probably taking in a double feature. Kate put Daniel Messenger firmly from her mind, and turned to *Daniel Deronda.*

chapter 9

JERRY was not at a double feature. It would have annoyed him to know that Kate thought he might be; but his annoyance would have been nothing to Kate's had she known what he was up to. He was, in fact, lying in wait for Emanuel.

It was not precisely that Jerry doubted Kate's assurances of Emanuel's innocence. The two of them, Jerry knew, had been friends, and, Jerry suspected, something more—though Kate had been rather vague on this point—and this said a good deal for Emanuel's innocence, since women, Jerry believed, did not automatically have a high opinion of men they had loved but not married. Nonetheless, to Jerry's masculine, therefore objective, intelligence, Emanuel was still Number One as a suspect, and the fact that Kate was convinced of his innocence did not weigh as much with Jerry as he had pretended. Although he was prepared to follow Kate's instructions—she was, after all, paying him—he could carry them out with a greater sense of single purpose if he had met, and talked with, Emanuel. Jerry had, at almost twenty-two, great faith in his ability to size people up.

It was not possible, of course, simply to go in and present himself to Emanuel as Kate's assistant and nephew-to-be. In the first place, Kate had not told Emanuel about his, Jerry's, part in the investigations; and in the second place, it was important to catch Emanuel off his guard. For one thing, he wanted to know if Emanuel, with the eleven o'clock hour now free, would simply wander out, as Kate and Nicola had been sure he would.

Jerry therefore provided himself with a chamois from a Madison Avenue store—he righteously did not enter this on his expense account—and stood across the street from the entrance to Emanuel's office polishing a car. This gave him a fine view of anyone who went out or in, and also a reason for loitering on an elegant street where people were not encouraged to loiter. It would be inconvenient if the owner of the car appeared, but Jerry was prepared to cope with this.

At five to eleven a young man emerged from the building. Richard Horan, in all probability. Jerry, ducking behind the car to wipe the fender, got a long look at him. Mr. Horan would have to be encountered later in the day. Rather to Jerry's surprise, Mr. Horan looked like Hollywood's idea of a "young Madison Avenue executive on his way up"; because Horan was in analysis, Jerry realized that he had expected him to look a bit more harried and uncertain, the Brooks Brothers suit perhaps askew. But here was assurance personified. Jerry felt a surge of relief, the origin of which he did not question; in fact, he was, without knowing it, glad that he did not have to pity Mr. Horan.

Once the object of his scrutiny had disappeared, appropriately enough, in the direction of Madison Avenue, Jerry continued to polish the car, though less assiduously, pausing to smoke a cigarette. He saw one woman enter, and one woman leave, presumably on their way to and from Dr. Barrister's office. To his surprise, neither of the women could be described as "aged." One of them, in fact, was considerably younger than Kate, whom Jerry thought of, though he would have died rather than admit it to her, as middle-aged. (Kate, of course, had had far too much experience with students of Jerry's age not to know precisely how he thought of her.) He forced himself to wipe the entire side of the car carefully, and to smoke a cigarette in an exaggeratedly leisurely fashion, before facing the fact of what was to be done next. He had just about decided that he had better go in and spin some sort of tale to Emanuel, when Emanuel himself, smoking a cigarette, came out of the doorway and turned toward the park.

Jerry could not, of course, be certain that this was Emanuel, but the man was the right age and was, moreover, wearing extremely shabby clothes, such as were unlikely to be worn by any tenant of so excellent a building except this eccentric man who donned old clothes for the purpose of running around the reservoir. Jerry folded his chamois neatly and left it on the fender as part payment to the owner of the car for the use that had been made of it, and followed the man into the park.

It was by no means clear to Jerry what he intended to do next. Trot around the reservoir after the man, trip him up perhaps, and then slip, amid apologies, into a conversation? Emanuel was certainly no fool; could Jerry get away with that? Perhaps, at the reservoir, something would present itself. One thing was clear: this man walked with urgency, with the physical energy of one who has sat too long, who needs, quite simply, to move. This explained why he would go to the trouble of changing his clothes for scarcely half an hour's run.

But he was destined not to have the run. He slowed down on one of the paths, so that Jerry came dangerously close to him. What had stopped him was a woman—who could tell what age?—over-made-up, appearing, appallingly, on the edge of lunacy. She was weeping, and the mascara ran in black streaks down her aging face, mingling with the rouge. Others saw her, some smirked, most simply turned away and skirted the path to avoid her. Jerry's instinct was to do the same.

But Emanuel stopped. "Can I help you?" he asked the woman. Jerry dropped, unnoticed, onto a bench behind Emanuel. The woman eyed her interlocutor with suspicion.

"I've lost him," she whimpered, "I just dozed off, and he's gone away. I don't sleep well at night."

"Your little boy?" Emanuel asked.

She nodded. "I tied his leash to the bench, but he must have pulled it loose. Cyril darling, come to Mama," she began to call. "Don't you hurt him," she said to Emanuel.

"How big was he?" Emanuel asked. "What color?" The scene, to Jerry, was grotesque. But Emanuel put his hand on the woman's arm. "What color was he?" he asked again. The gesture seemed to calm her.

"Brown," she said. "This big," and she made a movement, as of one who holds a small dog under one arm. She looked at the empty arm with love.

"He won't have gone far," Emanuel said. By this time they had collected a small and interested crowd. Emanuel began to search in the nearby bushes, and a few other men, with a shrug to show they thought this all non-

86

sense, joined him. Jerry forced himself to keep his seat. It was one of the other men who, perhaps five minutes later, found the dog, not far off, rolling in some indescribable, to him delightful, mess. A pleasant change after that woman, Jerry thought.

The woman retrieved the dog, scolding him, calling him a naughty, naughty boy, and walking away from Emanuel as though he were a tramp who had accosted her. The man who had found the dog pointed to his forehead meaningfully. Emanuel nodded, and looked at his watch. No time now for even the quickest run. He has a patient at twelve, Jerry thought, and he has to change his clothes. Emanuel began walking slowly back toward the avenue. Jerry did not follow; he remained on the bench, thinking about Richard Horan. The need to speak to Emanuel had evaporated, somehow, in the morning air.

After sitting for half an hour longer in the park, Jerry found himself viewing the profession of detective with somewhat less insouciance than he had felt that morning. In fact, he thought himself rather a fool. It was all very well to tell Kate, in his most debonair manner, that he was going down to apply for a job at the advertising agency where Richard Horan worked, but as an idea, this was several light-years away from being brilliant. Well, he might not apply for a job, but obviously the thing to do was to go down to the agency's offices and look around. It might work out that the best plan would be to follow Mr. Horan home—Jerry did not linger too long over the question of where, if anywhere, this would lead—but he might just as well move now in the general direction of Horan.

Going downtown in the Madison Avenue bus, Jerry pulled out the picture of the young man and studied it. Could it possibly be a picture of Horan? Viewing his victim from behind the car fender, Jerry had had only a general impression; a detailed description of the man's face had not remained with him. Surely a detective who has had one look at a man should never again forget the face; Jerry, far from forgetting it, had really nothing to remember. Still, he felt, swallowing his humility, it was fairly certain that Horan had not looked like this. Well, one could but make sure.

It is one of the odd tricks of fate that, when we have admitted ourselves to be foolish, fully to blame for our own mistakes, she will hand us a piece of good fortune on a platter. The Greeks, of course, understood all about this, but Jerry had yet to learn it. Years later, Jerry was to look back on this as the time when he had learned that though one must do all one can, success is never entirely the result of one's own efforts. Yet now, emerging from the bus, he knew only his own inadequacy.

All advertising agencies were named, by Jerry, Bing, Bang, Bilge and Oblivion. This particular Bing, Bang, etcetera, had its offices on the eighteenth floor. Jerry stepped from the elevator feeling rather as though he were going into orbit. Surely there would be a receptionist. But Jerry was never to know whether there was or not. A hand was placed on his shoulder; in that moment, Jerry was certain, his hair began to go gray.

"What are you doing here? Don't tell me Sally's talked you into going into the advertising racket. Take my advice; stick to the law."

It was Horan. Jerry stared at him open-mouthed, as though he were an alligator who had appeared suddenly in a suburban bathtub.

"You are the Jerry who's engaged to Sally Fansler, no? I met you at a party. . . . Anything wrong?" Jerry looked, in fact, as though he were going to faint.

"Small world," he managed to say. "To coin a phrase," he added, trying to save himself from the monstrous ineptitude of the first cliché.

"I think it is, literally. In my opinion, there are only fifty people in the world, and they keep moving about. Have you had lunch?"

Dear, wonderful, blessed Sally, who really did know everybody. Jerry had realized, in a vague sort of way, that this might be useful—he was thinking years ahead to his practice of law—but now he began to view Sally's connections in an even brighter light. He had often remarked to Sally, jokingly, that he thought they read different editions of the *Times* each morning. She never glanced at the sports page; Africa, the Near East, Russia, the acts of Congress whirled about somewhere in the outer reaches of her consciousness; if, to save her life, she had to name the nine justices of the Supreme Court, she would mention Warren, and die. But for her the *Times* was filled with small news items of people changing jobs, marrying, divorcing, supporting causes, and none of these items was ever forgotten. She not only "knew everybody" through the vast connections of family, school, college, dates—her social world generally—she also knew all about them.

"My brother Tom used to date Sally," Horan was saying, as, in a dream, they stepped back into the elevator. "What are you doing these days?"

At lunch, Jerry allowed Horan to buy him a Gibson. He was not used to drinking in the middle of the day, but this, after all, was in the nature of forcing brandy down the throat of an injured man. Even through an alcoholic haze, it was brilliantly clear that Horan did not resemble the man whose picture was now in the inside pocket of Jerry's jacket. Furthermore, could anyone from Sally's world stab a girl on a couch? Not in a fit of passion, but in a coolly calculated crime?

"You in analysis?" Jerry asked. He heard the words with horror. He had meant, by the most devious circumlocution, to lead up to the subject. He ought not to have had the Gibson. What a detective he was making. Jerry stuffed his mouth with some bread, hoping, not too scientifically, that it would soak up the alcohol.

It was Horan's turn to look shocked. "My God!" he said, "where did you hear that?"

"Oh, I didn't," Jerry said with a wave of his hand. "Just one of these things one says these days, you know, just to throw it on the stoop to see if the cat will sniff it." He smiled encouragingly.

Horan looked like a man who, stooping to pet a dog, discovers it to be a hyena. The arrival of the food provided a fortunate interlude. Jerry began to eat rather rapidly. "Sorry," he finally murmured.

Horan waved a forgiving hand. "I *am* in analysis, as a matter of fact. It's not exactly a secret. As a matter of fact, my analyst is the man who just had a girl murdered on his couch."

"Have you continued with him anyway?" Jerry ingenuously asked.

"Why not? Of course, he didn't do it; at least, I don't think he did. My family thinks I should quit, but what the hell, you can't run out on every sinking ship. To coin a phrase," he added.

"Did you know the girl?" Having begun with direct questions, Jerry thought it best thus to continue.

"No, I didn't, more's the pity. I used to see her in the waiting room when I came out, but I didn't even know her name. Damn good-looking. I told her once that I just happened to have two tickets to a show that night, and would she like to go—as a matter of fact, I'd bought them that morning from a scalper—but she wasn't having any. Cold sort of fish. Odd, just the same, that someone should have murdered her."

It had, hideously, the ring of truth. But surely murderers were good liars.

"Is your analyst a good one?" Jerry asked.

"Highly recommended. He's perfectly willing to sit there for twenty minutes if I don't open my mouth. Apparently I'm resenting him, though. Dream I had." Jerry looked interested. "You're supposed to tell them your dreams, of course; never thought I dreamt much, but you do, if you make yourself remember them. Well, in this dream I was in Brooks Brothers buying a suit. The suit seemed to be damned expensive, but I got it anyway, and when I tried it on at home it didn't fit at all. I took it back to the store, and got into a violent argument with the salesman about how I'd been overcharged, and the goddam suit wasn't worth a nickel. I woke up in a fury, and rushed off to tell Dr. Bauer about it. Well, it seems it was quite a simple dream. I was resenting him, Dr. Bauer, and thought he was cheating me in charging so much for just listening to me talk, but it wasn't a thought I'd wanted to face, so I dreamt about it in that way. Clever, huh?"

It was undoubtedly magnificent as a lesson in analytic technique, but for Jerry's purposes it was worthless. Or could one resent an analyst enough to try to frame him for murder? An interesting thought. Jerry wondered if analysts ever thought of it as one of the risks of their profession. Not a bad motive, now that Jerry came to consider it. He wondered, fleetingly, how Kate was doing with Frederick Sparks.

"Don't misunderstand me," Jerry said, "but did you ever feel you'd like to kill Dr. Bauer?"

"Not *kill* him," Horan answered, apparently unoffended

by the question, "though God knows what goes on in one's murky unconscious. One fantasizes about one's analyst of course, but mostly it's picturing oneself running into someone who knows him and finding out all the grisly secrets of his life, or having him drop the professional airs and beg one for help. One of the most maddening things about an analyst is that you tell him a joke, even a damn funny joke, and there's nothing in back of you but silence. I wonder if, that night, he says to his wife—I assume he's married—'Heard a damn funny joke today from one of my patients.' "

"Is he helping you with whatever problem you went to him for?"

"Well, not yet of course, but it's still early. We've uncovered a lot of interesting material. For one thing, even though I don't remember it, it turns out I knew all the time that my mother was pregnant with my brother. Analysis has already helped me with my work."

"Did you have a block of some sort?"

"Not that way. One of our clients makes elegant furniture, and I thought up an ad of a room with just two pieces of furniture in it, the couch and the chair behind it, each of them perfect pieces of furniture, of course. Got quite a nice pat on the head for that."

Horan went on to talk about nonanalytic matters, and it was beyond Jerry's powers even to try to bring him back to the subject for which he had sought him out. He seemed, in any case, most unlikely as a murderer. Perhaps he had hired someone to do the job; but, the world of organized crime apart, was that really possible? And did Horan know anything about the way Emanuel's complicated domestic arrangements worked out? That uncertainty about whether or not Emanuel had a wife might have been a clever blind. Still, could anyone seem, like Horan, so exactly what he was, and not be?

Jerry parted from Horan, who had paid for the lunch, with a feeling of depression and a splitting headache. What could he do between now and the off-duty time of Dr. Barrister's pretty nurse? After a few moments' fruitless contemplation, Jerry went to a double feature.

chapter 10

JERRY emerged, like a groundhog, from his place of hibernation into the sunlight. He had seen halves of two movies, and had only the haziest idea of what either was about, but he suspected that the two halves combined made a more interesting movie than either of them whole would have done. His mind, in any case, had been on other things. Why, for example, had he not asked Richard Horan about telephone calls to Emanuel's office? If Horan had arranged for those phone calls canceling the appointments, he might, in his confusion at Jerry's question, have indicated it. On the other hand, if Horan had paid someone to make the calls, Jerry's mentioning them would have put Horan, who seemed at any rate to have no suspicions about Jerry—apart from those about his sanity—on his guard. It seemed to Jerry that being a detective involved, more than any other profession, the constant traveling up dead-end roads. And no one, of course, ever bothered to put up signs on the roads saying Dead End.

Jerry, worried lest he miss Dr. Barrister's nurse, took a taxi from the movie theater to the office where, all unknowingly, she awaited (he hoped) his arrival. He had spent none of Kate's money and an uncomfortably large chunk of his own. He could not, in decency, charge Kate for the chamois, or the movie, or the taxi the movie had necessitated. Well, perhaps he could charge her for the chamois—after all, without that previous glimpse of Horan he would not have recognized him in the advertising office—which would have made, of course, no difference whatever. In the movie, however—and with this Jerry consoled himself—he had worked out a plan for approaching the nurse. That the plan would, had she known of it, have given Kate the screaming heebie-jeebies, could not, in this moment of desperation, deter Jerry for an instant.

The sign outside Dr. Barrister's office read: Ring and walk in. Jerry did so. The nurse was there, working at a typewriter, alone. "Yes?" she said to Jerry, obviously mystified at his presence, his sex, and his errand. Seen this close, she was neither as young nor as pretty as Jerry had thought.

"It's about my wife," Jerry said. He sounded, to himself, extremely unconvincing, but hoped the nurse would put it down to uxorial nervousness. The nurse seemed undecided whether to laugh or call the police. "She, that is, we, that is—we wanted to have a baby. Is it all right if I sit down?" he added, doing so.

"The doctor isn't here," the nurse said, and then immediately regretted, it was clear from her expression, having admitted the fact to this lunatic. She barricaded herself behind an official attitude. "If your wife cares to call and make an appointment, or if you wish to make one now . . ." She took an appointment book from her desk and hovered over it, pen in hand. "Who recommended you to Dr. Barrister?" she horribly asked.

It was then that Jerry marshaled his by no means negligible reserve of charm. That he looked harried from his afternoon's experiences, he did not doubt. Omitting his usual restraining gesture, he allowed the forelock of his hair to drop forlornly over his forehead. He smiled at her with the smile that no female, since he was four, had been able to resist. The desolate slump of his body, the sorrow in his eyes, the smile, all indicated that here, all unhoped for, was a woman who could understand him. He became, all of him, an appeal from the depths of masculine helplessness to the heights of female competence and comfort. The nurse, though she did not know it, dropped her weapons and retired, joyfully defeated, from the field. She was far from insensitive to masculine attentions, and competent only in dealing with troubled women, whom she cowed. For the first time that day, Jerry was in control of a situation.

"Alice, my wife, was very nervous about coming here. But, of course, she ought to see a doctor. So I had to promise"—his look included the nurse in some all-encompassing understanding of women—"that I would come first and see that the doctor was a sympathetic sort of person. Alice is shy. But I'm sure if I tell her how very nice you are, and that you will of course treat her gently, I'll be able to persuade her to come. I'm sure you must have lots of women with her problem here. That must be mainly what you do, isn't it?"

"Well, we *do* do that, of course. And then there are older women with various—um—problems. . . ." The nurse seemed to search her mind for the most presentable of these. "Problems of—well—change of life, and that sort of thing."

"Of course," Jerry said, with a great air of comprehension, though his ignorance of this subject could scarcely have been purer. "Is there something you can do for that?" This question was most unnatural for a young husband, a reluctant non-father, to ask, but Jerry hoped it would go down. The nurse, her attention not on the subject of the conversation, but on its quality, swallowed the question easily. "Oh, there's a great deal you can do," she said, twiddling her pen prettily, "there are hormone injections, and pills, and, of course, the attentions of a competent physician." She smiled. "And then, women have other silly feminine complications."

Jerry tucked this information neatly away for future reference. "But you do," he earnestly asked, "treat women who want to have babies?"

"Oh, yes, of course. There are many treatments that help a great deal. And Dr. Barrister is very understanding."

"I'm glad to hear that," Jerry said. "Because Alice would require an understanding sort of person. Would you call Dr. Barrister 'fatherly'?"

The nurse seemed disconcerted by the word. "Well, no, not exactly *fatherly*. But he's very competent, and calm and helpful. I'm sure your wife will like him. But you know," she mischievously added, "you'll have to go somewhere to be tested too. I mean, it isn't *always* the woman's fault, you know."

Jerry decided to allow this to embarrass him. He looked down, ordered the forelock to fall, and coughed. "Perhaps Alice could come Friday?" he asked nervously.

"The doctor isn't here on Friday," the nurse said. "Some other day?" To Jerry, thinking of the porter's stolen uniform, this confirmation was satisfying, but less so than it might have been had it not reminded him that he had forgotten to ask Horan where *he* was last Friday. "Perhaps I'd better have Alice call," he said, rising to his feet. "You've been very nice. Is—er—I was wondering—is Dr. Barrister very—are his fees very high?"

"Yes, I'm afraid so," the nurse said. "You can't have been married very long," the nurse kindly added. "Perhaps you oughtn't to worry yet."

"You know how women are," Jerry said. "Thank you again."

"Not at all," the nurse said, as he closed the door. Jerry rushed to Fifth Avenue and grabbed another taxi, which he would definitely charge to Kate. Sally expected him. He felt that the interview with the nurse had gone extremely well, but what, in the name of all gynecologic mysteries, had he found out?

As Jerry sped Sally-ward in his taxi, Kate, having seen Daniel Deronda off on his Zionist dream, was also in a taxi, moving toward the building Jerry had just left. She had telephoned Emanuel and Nicola and discovered that the six o'clock patient had canceled, whether because he was retreating from the field or having the usual psycho-analytic misgivings was not altogether clear. "You had better come over," Nicola had said on the phone, "and we will all sit on Emanuel's couch to make sure no one else leaves a body there." Nicola had also, after a good deal of broad hinting from Kate, extended an invitation to dinner.

Kate found them in the living room, where, they had decided, they could watch the entrance to the office and prevent the intrusion of any bodies. Kate put her package, obviously a bottle, down on the table. "Not for you," she said to Nicola. "It's for a party where I am going later to meet Frederick Sparks." She caught Emanuel's eye. "Did Janet Harrison, in her hours with you, ever mention Daniel Messenger?" Kate asked.

"The police have already asked me that," Emanuel said.

"Oh, dear, I keep forgetting about the police. Are they getting restive?"

"Well," Nicola said, "this Daniel Messenger is a help, whoever he is. I got out of one of those detectives that he's a geneticist, at least that's what Emanuel says he sounds like from my rather garbled description; but apparently he's involved in studying some mysterious disease that only Jews get, or that only Jews don't get, in some Italian (I think) places, and apparently if they can find the clue to this evasive tolerance or intolerance they'll know something more about heredity. As to whether they, the police, believe that Emanuel and I never heard of him, who, including the police, can tell?"

Kate looked at Emanuel. "She never mentioned him, I take it, or any theories about genes?" Emanuel shook his head. Kate saw that he was becoming depressed, and her heart went out to him, but there was little, except helping Nicola to babble at him, that she could do. Nicola's mother, Kate learned, had carried the children off to her country home. They had been hearing too much here, and allowing them to go a week after the murder did not seem so much a capitulation before the fates.

"Dr. Barrister doesn't have office hours on Fridays, is that right?" Kate asked Nicola.

"No," Nicola said. "Why?"

"I have come to ask questions," Kate said sententiously, "not to answer them."

"Are there any questions left to ask?" Emanuel said.

"Very many," Kate said firmly. "But you are *not* to repeat any of them to the police. Or to anyone else," she added firmly, looking at Nicola. "Here are some questions: Who stole the porter's uniform on the morning Janet Harrison's room was robbed?" Emanuel and Nicola both stared at her in astonishment, but she hurried on. "Why was her room robbed? Was it merely as some idiot suggested, that a frustrated man wanted one of her more intimate garments?"

"Are you drunk?" Emanuel asked.

"Don't interrupt. If that is so, who is this man? Why did Janet Harrison make a will? It's rather an odd thing for an unmarried young woman to do. Who is Daniel Messenger, that she should will to him, or he to her? Although your erstwhile patient, Emanuel, seems to have led a most circumspect life, to put it mildly, she was seen with a man. Who was he? Who saw her?"

"If you don't know who saw her, how do you know she was seen?" Nicola asked.

"Stop interrupting. You may take notes, or just listen, but let me finish. I am organizing my thoughts. Why did Janet Harrison decide to study English literature when she had started in history, with a bypath into nursing? Why nursing? Why did she come to New York to study English literature?"

"That's easy," Emanuel said. "She knew there was a charming lunatic named Kate Fansler teaching there."

Kate ignored him. "What worried Janet Harrison about the present? What worried her about the past? Who is the young man whose picture she cherished and hid? Did the police show you that? You didn't recognize it. Neither has anyone else. Why? Or rather, why not? What about Richard Horan? What about Frederick Sparks? What about the window cleaner?"

"Window cleaner?"

"Well, it just occurred to me, perhaps a window cleaner, who might have some sort of *thing* about women on couches, who knew her from cleaning the office windows when she was there, or the waiting rooms windows while she was waiting, had observed the routine of your house, and stabbed her one day when he happened to glance in on his way to clean someone else's windows, and had perhaps by now forgotten the whole thing. Who cleans your windows?"

If her object had been to distract Emanuel, she had succeeded. He laughed, and went to get them all a drink. "The office windows aren't ever cleaned when patients are there," Nicola said. "And anyway, we don't have a window cleaner. Pandora does them. There's no danger of falling out, you know, and, in any case, the outside ones are done by the house, because they are a special job owing to the bars across them. But *do* explain all your other fascinating questions. How do you know Frederick Sparks?"

"I don't know him."

"Then why are you going to a party with him?"

"Because I am Kate Fansler, the great detective," she said. Yet suddenly she thought: It's all very well, there are a lot of questions and they add up nicely, but shall we ever find the answers? And why did Emanuel's six o'clock patient cancel? That was, perhaps, the most important question of them all. Having lifted Emanuel from

97

the pit of despair, she was about to tumble into it herself when the telephone rang. "It's for you, Kate," Emanuel called from the kitchen.

"But nobody knows I'm here," Kate said, taking up the phone.

"I guessed," came Reed's voice, "when there was no answer at home. Can you have dinner?"

"I'm having dinner here. Then I'm going to a party to meet Frederick Sparks."

"Why not take me along? Together, we'll turn him inside out."

"Nonsense, I'll do better myself. If you're there, and everybody discovers you're an Assistant District Attorney, we'll spend the evening discussing why so many people bribe policemen. You forget, I've been to parties with you before."

"All right, you ungrateful wretch, then I'll have to give you my great piece of news over the phone. I hope I can conclude that no one but you can hear the sound of my voice."

"Oh, quite."

"Good. Dr. Michael Barrister was once sued for malpractice. It had the looks of quite a nasty case, but was apparently settled. Of course, doctors carry malpractice insurance."

"What had he done?"

"Apparently some woman began to grow hair on her chest. Years ago, of course."

"Are you trying to be funny?"

"I couldn't be that funny, even if I tried. Remember, Kate, it probably doesn't mean a thing. The patient in the case had no connection with Janet Harrison. But I thought it might encourage you to know that at least someone in this benighted case has a blot on his escutcheon."

"Reed! Does this mean they're really starting to look elsewhere?"

"Let's say I'm encouraging them. But don't get your hopes up. It's a big step from hormones to a knife plunged home."

"Thanks, Reed. I'm sorry about tonight."

"I should hope so," said Reed, and hung up.

When they sat down to dinner, Kate asked Emanuel to explain to her about hormones. He began by saying he knew very little about it, he hadn't followed developments in the field since his days at medical school, and then he began, as only Emanuel could, to discourse on the subject. At first Kate understood every third word, and then she understood every sixth, and then she caught only a familiar conjunction every dozen words or so, and then she stopped listening. If this case is going to require a detailed knowledge of endocrinology, she thought, I'd better give up right now. Yet, even at that moment, the telephone was ringing in her apartment, peal after unanswered peal, only mildly frustrating to one with a message which was to mark, for the three of them at the dinner table, and for one other, the beginning of the end.

chapter 11

FROM the moment when Kate, bottle in hand, arrived at the party, she felt like someone at an amusement park being thrust on one dizzy ride after another. She met her host for only a moment when he seized the bottle, thanked her, and introduced, inaudibly, four or five people standing about. These glanced at Kate, decided she was a specimen of which they already had a sufficient number in their collection, and went on discussing some intramural college fight the central issue of which, if there was one, Kate did not manage to grasp. Lillian had warned her that when members of this department got together, they never discussed anything but department politics, the exigencies of the teaching schedule, the insufficiencies of the administration and the peculiarities—moral, physical, psychological and sexual—of certain absent members. What Kate was not prepared for was the violence with which all these things were discussed, the enthusiasm with which points were made which must certainly, it seemed, have been made before.

Several aspects of the gathering surprised Kate not at all. One was the amount of alcoholic stimulation which members of the academic profession could withstand. They were by no means constant drinkers, but as members of an underpaid profession, they drank whenever they got the chance. This had long since been discovered by textbook publishers, whose habit it was, at any official academic convention, to rent a room and hand round the drinks with a free hand. Nor was Kate surprised that literature was nowhere being discussed. People whose profession was the study of literature did not discuss it when they foregathered, unless the question concerned the constitution of courses or the assignment of them. The reasons for this were obscure and complex, and Kate had never thoroughly analyzed them. She had been present with enough groups of doctors, lawyers, economists, sociologists and others to know that it took the talents of a Svengali to get them to talk about anything at all besides their subjects.

Yet the people here suffered, apparently, from the fact that they were employed not by an educational institution, but by a bureaucratic system. They were all, to a large extent, clerks, neatly bound up in red tape, and, like clerks, they gave themselves the illusion of freedom by discussing and ridiculing the strictures that bound them. Kate thought lovingly of her own university, where one struggled, God knew, against the ancient sins of favoritism, flattery and simony, but where the modern horrors of bureaucracy had not yet strangled her colleagues or herself.

"My final exam in 3.5," one young man was saying, "was scheduled for the last day of the exam period, and they wanted the marks in within twenty-four hours. I pointed out that I could not possibly read thirty-five examinations with anything approaching fairness, let alone intelligence, and why couldn't I get the grades in three days later? Do you know what the dean of Utter Confusion said—actually said—sitting there in his huge office, while the faculty, of course, far from having an office, can't even find a drawer in which to place their private belongings? He said, 'But the IBM machines must begin to operate twenty-four hours after the exam period is over.' The IBM machines. Why? I ask you, why? But at least I discovered whom the college is run for. One knew, of course, that it wasn't run for the students or the faculty; after all, this isn't Oxford or Cambridge. I had thought it was run for the administration, or the building and grounds committee. But no! It's run for the IBM machines. Do you know, when I was filling out all those atrocious little grade cards for the IBM machine, with that revolting little pencil one has to use, I wanted to write F——— Y—— right across the damn thing, and see what the IBM machine would make of that, the cybernetic little bastard!"

"That's nothing. The other day I got one of those aptitude exam results, all figured out by machine, and that

101

idiotic student counselor . . ." Kate moved off in the direction of Fredrick Sparks, slowly, for she didn't want to appear to have been stalking him. Lillian had pointed him out to her. He sat back in his chair, glass in hand, observing the room with the pleasant superiority of one who has emerged successful from the struggle for tenure, and has not yet dropped, screaming, into the pit where promotion is fought for.

Kate sat down on the chair next to him, for most people, the better to make their points, were standing; she asked him, with a regrettable lapse of originality, for a match. He produced an elegant lighter and lit her cigarette with a flourish.

"Are you a friend of Harold's?" he asked. But apparently he accepted the fact that she must be, for he went on to ask if she taught, and where. Kate told him. He expressed envy. Kate, with some dishonesty, asked why she was to be envied. "I'll give you an example," he said, swinging around in his chair to face her. "How many mimeographed communications have you received so far this semester?"

"Mimeographed communications? Oh, I don't know. Four or five, I guess, perhaps more. Announcements of department meetings, and that sort of thing. Why do you ask?"

"Because I have had hundreds, hundreds, thousands, perhaps, by now, and so has everyone else. Not only announcements of committee meetings to discuss every conceivable and inconceivable subject upon the face of the earth, but announcements from the administration: all students wearing shorts or blue jeans must be reported; the faculty is reminded that smoking is *not* permitted on the stairs (this of course is a cozy one, because if a man and woman faculty member want to have five minutes' conversation, and happen to be smokers, they must either retire to the faculty lounge, which is a nest of political intrigue, and in any case is usually given over to some student function, or they can one or the other indulge in transvestism and retire to the men's or ladies' room, as the case might be, because smoking is allowed there, or they can smoke on the stairs, which is what they do). *Or,* there may be an announcement that the pencil sharpener has been moved to Room 804 (if not out of the building altogether). *Or,* there may be an announcement the garbage will now be collected from the courtyard immediately outside the classroom windows every afternoon from one to five. The administration realizes that this will make teaching practically impossible (have you ever heard the noise of a garbage truck close up?), but the faculty must learn which are the important problems in the running of a college. I once got a mimeographed atrocity asking me to come and discuss methods of giving the faculty more time for original work. I wrote back that the best way *I* could think of was not to hold meetings discussing it. As I say, I envy you."

"I hear you're to be congratulated on getting tenure."

"Where did you hear that? I'm not to be congratulated; I'm to be pitied. Gustave is pleased because we now know we shall eat regularly, and retire on a pension; but if I had an ounce of guts I would say: 'You idiots, don't give me tenure; I am already dreadfully inclined to indolence, lassitude, self-indulgence and procrastination. You have enough dead wood in this benighted institution, enough minds which have not been penetrated by a new thought since the possibility of nuclear fission filtered through; but, no, you are a political institution; you must offer me what the masses crave: security.' Of course, it is possible that I shall succeed. That I shall break out from the bounds of faculty life."

"Write a great book?"

"No. Become a member of the administration. Then I shall have a carpet, a whole desk to myself, and perhaps one for my secretary, a larger salary and the right to be nostalgic about teaching. Will you have another drink?"

"That, at least, is the same at my institution," said Kate, declining the drink with a shake of her head. "As somebody said, the reward for teaching well is to stop teaching." Kate was not really fooled by his manner. Beneath the gabble of exaggeration, and the chi-chi reference to his dog (she should really have asked, "But who is Gustave?"), Kate suspected a first-rate brain and a daunted personality. She had no doubt he possessed the guts, the brains and the egoism essential to the stabbing of anyone, but had he done it? Ardent lovers of dogs are frequently those who cannot bear any less than an unquestioning love. He would certainly have had the nerve to make those phone calls. Could he have been attracted to Janet Harrison, largely because she was noncommunicative and withdrawn, and then have offered love, to have it rejected? "How many days a week do you teach?" she asked.

"Four, God help me. And next semester it may well be five. This semester I happen, through the queerest chance of fate, to have Monday off."

"Do you teach in the mornings on all the other days?" Kate hoped the question did not sound as pointed to him as it did to her.

"I will show you my schedule," he said, reaching into an inner pocket. "You might think that this late in the year I would know my schedule. But, in fact, our schedules are so complicated that if I were to commit this to memory it would take up so much space in my meager brain that I would forget something else, like Anglo-Saxon." He handed her the schedule.

It was indeed extraordinary. He taught a course labeled 9.1 at nine on Tuesday, three on Wednesday, ten on Thursday, and ten (!) on Friday. Kate asked the reason for this oddity, while thinking, Here is an alibi, clear and straightforward.

"Oh, but it's very simple, really, provided you have the peculiarly inchoate mind of the man arranging these things. Some students are on P schedules, or Q, or S or W. This means they must swim at a certain time one day, and eat at a certain time on another, and on no condition be on the stairs at a certain time on the third. All this gets whirred around, and here we are. Sometimes it works out that a class will meet at one, and then again at three on the same afternoon. *There's* a pedagogical challenge, if you want one."

"Do you ever cut any classes?"

"Never, unless of course one is dying. If one simply *cannot* teach, one meets the little darlings, and then tells them to run along, Papa isn't feeling well today. Of course, since the state is paying for them, and not they or their fond parents, they scamper off overjoyed and certain they have got away with something. What you must *never* do is get a friend to take your classes. If the friend is seen (and we are thick with spies), it will be reported to Big

104

Brother, and both of you will have something to answer when you come before P. and B. You look, I am pleased to say, horrified. But the fact is that while the faculty is the only thing without which you cannot have a first-rate institution, it is the last element considered here. When, several years ago, polio shots became compulsory, they were given first to the administration, then to the kitchen staff, then to building and grounds, then to the students, and finally (always hoping there would be some serum left), to the faculty. The IBM machines would have got it first, had anyone been able to discover where to administer the injection."

On an impulse, Kate drew what she now thought of as *the* picture from her purse and handed it to Sparks. "Have you ever seen him?" she asked. "I thought perhaps he might have been a student here," she glibly lied.

Sparks took the picture and studied it with care. "I never forget a face," he said. "Not a boast, just a fact. But I never remember voices or names, which is, I am told, not insignificant. Do you know, I don't think I've met this chap, but I may have passed him on the stairs, or perhaps only gone up an elevator with him once in an office building. It's not the whole face though; the eyes are wrong. But the shape of it—well, it's no use, but if I think whom he reminds me of I'll let you know. Did you mislay him somehow?"

"Yes, as a matter of fact. I thought he might be connected with Janet Harrison, a student of mine."

"What! The young lady stabbed on the couch? I was there when they discovered her body, you know. Was she a student of yours?"

"You were *there?*"

"Yes. Bauer happens to be my analyst too. Speaking of faces, hers was extraordinary. I used to come early sometimes, if the damn subway didn't tie me up, just to look at it."

"Did you ever talk to her?"

"Certainly not. As I told you, I'm not much on voices, except my own, which I like to hear going on and on. Besides, suppose that face had turned out to have a squeaky, nasal voice? I could never have enjoyed it again. Tell me, by the way, did she?"

"Have a nasal voice? No. It was a quiet voice, yet nervous. Is Bauer a good analyst?"

"Oh, yes. First-rate. Excellent at hearing what one doesn't say, which with me, of course, is all-important." And suddenly, as though to give Kate the opportunity to hear what he did not say, he leaned back and literally vanished behind a curtain of silence. Kate, who disliked parties, and was tired, felt depressed. Reed had been right. Detective was not a game you played at because you admired Peter Wimsey, and had a friend in a fearful jam. She had crashed a party, cornered this man, bewildered Lillian, and all to what purpose? Did it signify that he was teaching at the hour after ten on the day when the uniform was stolen? He had kept his appointment with Emanuel. Could he possibly have got up to the women's dormitory to rob Janet Harrison's room? It seemed unlikely. Could he have hit out at this quiet girl because he loathed himself for succumbing to an institution he did not respect? You have developed quite a talent for questions, Kate told herself, but you have not found a single answer.

Kate said Good night and Thank you to her host, who clearly did not remember who she was, waved to Lillian, and found herself a taxi. What next? Supposedly Jerry would have got something from Horan, but was he likely to have got more from him than she had from Sparks? So help me, Kate thought, if this case is ever settled, I'll never ask another question apart from literature as long as I live!

Firm in this resolution, Kate paid off the taxi and entered the lobby of her house to find Reed asleep there on a chair. She woke him, none too gently.

"I wanted to see you," he said. "It seems to me that if you're trying to be a detective you ought to stay home and answer the telephone instead of drinking at parties, forcing yourself on people and asking idiotic questions."

"I agree with you," Kate said, leading him into the apartment.

"Let me make some coffee," Reed said.

"Why all this solicitude? I'll make *you* some coffee."

"Sit down. I'll put up the coffee and then I want to talk to you. Two more things have come up—one is fascinating, though I'll be damned if I can make any sense

106

of it, and the other is a little frightening. I'll take the frightening one first." Maddeningly, he vanished into the kitchen, where Kate followed him.

"What is it? I've been sitting down all evening. Is Emanuel in more trouble?"

"No. You are."

"I?"

"How wonderful to be a professor of English! Anyone else would have said 'Me?' The police have received a letter, Kate. Anonymous, of course, and impossible to trace, but they don't pay as little attention to these things as they would like people to think. It's quite coherently written, and accuses you of murdering Janet Harrison."

"Me?"

"It claims, one, that the article you published a month ago in some learned journal or other on James's use of the American heroine was written by, and stolen from, Janet Harrison. You had not published enough, and were concerned about your career. It claims, two, that you and Emanuel were lovers, that you are still in love with him, resented his marriage to Nicola, and planned to get rid of the girl who was a threat, and to ruin Emanuel and incidentally Nicola, whom you loathe. It points out further that you have no alibi, know the Bauer home intimately, and knew the girl well enough to get her confidence and sit behind her. It makes a few other accusations, but those are the main ones. Oh, and it does mention that you robbed her room to rid the place of any notes she might have made toward the article. Now, just calm down and listen to me a minute. It doesn't explain why you should have published the article and only got the wind up after the article had appeared. But it's a pretty cogent case, and the police are taking it with some seriousness. They have also noted that you spend a good deal of time at the Bauer house, possibly covering your tracks, and that you went tonight to meet Frederick Sparks because he may have seen something and you wanted to find out if he had."

"How do they know where I was tonight? Did you tell them?"

"No, my dear, I did not. They extracted that information, very cleverly, from the Bauers."

"Is that why you wanted to go to meet him with me?"

"No. I only heard about this later. Since I'm poking my nose into something which isn't my business, I can't get my information hot off the griddle. Let's have some coffee."

Kate touched his arm. "Reed, do you believe any of this?"

But he had placed the cups, saucers, spoons, sugar, cream and coffeepot on a tray and carried them off into the living room.

chapter 12

"Do you believe it, Reed? No, don't pour me any coffee, I couldn't possibly swallow it." Reed poured it, nonetheless, and placed it in front of her.

"I said my news was frightening; I didn't say it was terrifying. And if you ask me again if I believe it, I'll beat you. Quite apart from all other considerations, do you think I would help someone, even someone for whom I felt gratitude and affection, to cover up a murder? What is true is that I know you, and do not know Emanuel, and therefore understand a little better how you felt about wanting to help him. That's something, isn't it? Now, please, drink your coffee. Kate, Kate, please don't. As I shall point out in a minute, this is really the best break you've had so far, in your crusade for Emanuel. You didn't expect to fight dragons and not even scratch your finger, did you? Here, use mine. I have never understood why no woman ever has a handkerchief, except in her purse, which is usually in another room. And I haven't told you my fascinating bit of news yet."

"I'll be all right in a minute. And you know, the girl wasn't found, after all, anywhere near me. How Emanuel must feel—how completely betrayed by circumstances! And do you know the first thing I thought—the first horrible, sniveling, petty thought I had—What will this do to me at the university? Can they possibly want a professor who's been accused of murder? Yet it touches me nowhere as near as it touches Emanuel. Reed, who do you think sent the letter?"

"Ah, the wheels are beginning to go round again, glory be! That's exactly the point. You've frightened someone, my dear, and frightened them badly. Though we may, of course, be leaping to a conclusion in thinking that it's you who frightened them, simply because the anonymous letter concerns you. You may simply be the only available victim, the only one who combines all the necessary qualifications to make the letter stick, even for a moment. But they—I mean, of course, he or she, but the English language is sadly lacking a genderless singular pronoun (do you remember your teacher saying 'everyone will please carry his or her chair into the next room?')— where was I, yes, they-he-she is afraid that some of the threads which are so neatly tangled in our hands will suddenly form themselves into a rope. Now, the question before the house at the moment is, What threads have we, and can we even disentangle them before making them into so much as a piece of string?"

"Reed, you're being very nice. You are very nice, you know, though I may not have mentioned it before. There's something I think I ought to tell you."

"That sounds ominous. You are now going to confess to some incredible folly, after telling me how nice I am. What have you done?"

"Well, the fact is, I've hired Jerry."

"Jerry! Kate, don't tell me you've got involved with a private detective! That would muck things up properly."

"No, Jerry is a sort of Baker Street Irregular, and he's going to be my nephew."

"You can't mean you've hired a little boy! Really, Kate . . ."

"Don't be an idiot. How could a little boy be going to be my nephew?"

"I can't imagine. Perhaps your sister is planning to adopt him."

"Reed, do listen. Of course he isn't a little boy, and I haven't got a sister. But I have got a niece, and she's engaged to Jerry, who happens to be in between things, and could go around seeing people I couldn't see."

"You're not old enough to have a niece about to be married, or are they getting engaged at fourteen these days? And if you needed someone, what's wrong with me? Was being engaged to your niece a major qualification for the job?"

"Reed, do try to understand. You have a job, just as I do, and can't go moseying around all day, even if you would, which, given your job, you couldn't. Anyway, you wouldn't take orders from me; you would just sit around and argue."

"I should hope so. Kate, you aren't fit to be let out alone."

"I'm beginning to believe you. Nevertheless, if you can manage to keep quiet for the length of time it takes you to drink another cup of coffee, I'll tell you where Jerry and I have got so far. That is, I'll tell you what I know; Jerry doesn't report on today's activities till tomorrow morning. Then we can see where we are, and you can tell me your fascinating bit." And, beginning with a description of Jerry, she told him about the porter's uniform, which reminded her of her conversation with Jackie Miller, so she told him that too, and about her investigations among the university records, and about Sparks, and Jerry's plans for meeting Horan and the nurse.

Reed took it, all things considered, rather well. He mulled the facts—if they *were* facts, he assiduously pointed out—over in his mind. "You realize," he said, "that the unspeakable Jackie Miller may hold the key to the whole business, always supposing that someone did see Janet Harrison with a man, and that the man is somehow connected with this case, though that's an awfully large number of supposes. Meanwhile, let me add my information to yours. And don't get all excited when you hear it. It sounds marvelous, but the more you think of it, the less sense it makes. In fact, the more I think about this whole affair, the more disjointed it seems. And, my dear young woman, we will certainly have to discuss this whole Jerry business. How you could for a moment have considered hiring—I suppose that means you are paying him to get himself in trouble, and go about muddying the waters— how you could have considered . . ."

"What's your fascinating fact, Reed? Let's hear it, and consider it, and then, when we've discovered the whole thing is nonsense, we can argue over Jerry at breakfast— I'm assuming it will be breakfast time by then."

"Very well. I told you about Daniel Messenger."

"I know. He's doing something with Jewish genes."

"Kate, that settles it. I am going. You are going to have a good night's sleep, and sometime tomorrow when you are rested . . ."

"Sorry. You told me about Daniel Messenger, and . . ."

"I told you, though you were, as I remember, not prepared to accept the statement, that Dr. Messenger looked nothing like our man of the picture. We had sent a young detective out to interview the good doctor, and it seemed we had wasted the detective's time and the citizens' money. Messenger had never heard of Janet Harrison, had never heard of Emanuel Bauer, had no particular opinions about psychiatry, and had certainly not left Chicago within weeks of the murder. Moreover, he couldn't begin to guess why Janet Harrison should have left him her money, but he suggested that perhaps another Daniel Messenger was meant. This was, of course, nonsense. She had delineated him clearly enough—knew, for example, where and when he had his residency, what sort of work he was doing, and so on. The lawyer had advised her to include the man's address, age, etcetera, which she had done. No doubt in the world that he was the man.

"As you can see, Kate, a pretty problem, though typical of this whole infuriating case—and the young detective was about to call it a day when he thought of something so obvious that he will probably turn out to be a genius and go far in the world—all ideas of genius appearing obvious after the genius has thought of them. Naturally, the detective had a copy of the picture found in Janet Harrison's purse, to be certain that Daniel Messenger did not, by any possible stretch of the imagination, resemble it. And just before he parted from the doctor, on an impulse, though no one had thought to suggest it to him, he showed Messenger the picture. He showed it to him quite casually, apparently, and not expecting anything to come of it. 'You don't happen to know this man, I suppose,' he said, or something of the sort.

"It seems that Messenger stared at the picture for quite a while, so that the detective thought he had gone off into a trance—you know how long seconds can be when you're waiting for a reply—and then Messenger looked at the detective and said 'That's Mike.' "

"Mike?" Kate asked.

"Just what the detective said: 'Mike? Mike who?' And what do you think the doctor said?"

"Oh, goody, guessing games. I just love guessing games. How many guesses may I have, Daddy? What did he say, in heaven's name?"

112

" 'Mike who?' he said, 'Mike Barrister; we shared a room once, donkey's years ago.' "

"Mike Barrister!" Kate said. "Dr. Michael Barrister. Reed! There's the connection we've been waiting for. I *knew* sooner or later some of our stray facts had to fit together. Janet leaves her money to Messenger, Messenger used to know Michael Barrister, and Michael Barrister has the office across from Emanuel. Reed, it's beautiful."

"I know it's beautiful. For one blinding, flashing, all-over moment, it's beautiful. But after the ringing in your ears stops, and you start to think about it a little, it's still beautiful all right, but it doesn't mean a goddam thing."

"Nonsense, she was murdered for her money."

"Even supposing it was enough money to murder someone for—which I don't for a single second grant—who murdered her? Messenger didn't; he didn't leave Chicago. And even if we're prepared to fall back on the hired murderer, which you admit is ridiculous, the result of every investigation in the world proves Messenger is the last person in the world to have done such a thing. He didn't frantically need money, we know that much, with the cooperation of his bank. His wife works as a secretary, and while they aren't rich, they aren't desperate. Far from it, apparently, because they've been quietly saving for the college education of their daughters. They haven't extravagant tastes—their idea of a marvelous vacation is to go camping in the northern reaches of Michigan. They aren't in debt, unless you call a mortgage on their house a debt; in which case you've got several million future murderers in the United States.

"I know, Kate, your mind is moving toward your favorite candidate, Dr. Michael Barrister. We even know he was once sued for malpractice, though I've since learned that the great majority of such suits are quite unjustified, and that every doctor is as likely as not to tangle with some lunatic who resents the fact that he hasn't been given a miracle cure, or who's heard somewhere that this treatment should have been preferred to that. But even if the suit was justified, being sued for malpractice doesn't make you a murderer. And if it did, why should Barrister murder a girl he had never met in order to leave a not very large sum of money to a man he hasn't seen in donkey's years?"

"Maybe Barrister just wanted to get Emanuel into trouble; maybe for some crazy reason he hates Emanuel."

"Maybe he does, though it's hard to imagine why. All we know is that Emanuel didn't particularly take to *him*. But then what has Messenger got to do with it? Why does the fact we are so excited about—that Messenger and Barrister once knew each other—have any bearing on Barrister's feeling for Emanuel? Emanuel and Messenger don't know each other, nor, except for a fortuitous sharing of the same address, do Barrister and Emanuel. It's a lovely fact, Kate, but it gets us nowhere. Absolutely nowhere."

"Wait a minute, Reed, you're confusing me. I'll admit that Messenger, while helpful, isn't exactly clarifying. But we now know who the young man in the picture is. Why didn't *we* recognize him by the way?"

"I didn't recognize him because I've never seen him. And you did, partly. You said the picture reminded you of someone, remember? A man changes a lot in those years between not-yet-thirty and over forty. Remember, Messenger hadn't seen Barrister since, at least we don't think he had. He saw the young man he had shared a room with. If I showed you a picture of a girl you'd known in high school you'd probably say: Oh, yes, that's Sally Jones. She always wore tight sweaters, and lisped. But if I showed you a picture of Sally Jones today, you might very well tell me you didn't know who she was."

"All right, go on playing the devil's advocate. The fact still remains that Dr. Michael Barrister had the office across the hall, was the one to pronounce the girl dead —at least to Nicola—and all the time his picture was in the purse of the murdered girl."

"And was left there by the murderer."

"Who overlooked it; it was folded inside her license."

"Or who left it there purposely, to lead us to think exactly what you're thinking."

"Damn. Damn, damn, damn."

"I couldn't agree more. But something occurs to me. Sparks said the face looked familiar, if you reported correctly. Could Sparks have known who the picture was of, and left it there? He sounds a man who goes in for rather involved circumspection."

"Perhaps we should show Messenger a picture of Sparks. It might turn out they had played baseball together in the dear, dead days of boyhood. I didn't think to ask where Sparks had come from. Anyway, they might have gone to the same Boy Scout camp when Sparks was visiting a maiden aunt in Messenger's hometown."

"I don't see why Messenger should recognize everyone in the case, but I agree it might not be a bad idea to show him photographs of all of them, supposing we can get them."

"At least we are moving away from Emanuel, Reed. Although," she added, remembering Reed's first news that night, "we seem to be moving either toward me or toward complete chaos. Still, we are moving. What shall we do next? Of course, we've forgotten Horan; perhaps he killed her as part of some advertising campaign. And the connection between Barrister and Messenger is coincidence. After all, life is full of coincidence, as Hardy knew, though none of us like to admit it. Oh, dear, I am beginning to go round and round. Reed, one question, before I succumb to dizziness and sleep: Where *was* Barrister the morning of the murder? Did the police ever establish that exactly?"

"He was in his office, which was full of patients, some in the waiting room, some in examining rooms. His nurse, of course, was there too. I suppose now the whole thing will have to be gone into more carefully, though the police didn't seem to consider that he had an alibi, that he was, that is, absolutely and unarguably elsewhere. I'm beginning to get a little dizzy myself."

"Well, in the morning I'll hear from Jerry about Horan. And the nurse. Perhaps Jerry . . ."

"Oh, yes, we *must* discuss Jerry. Kate, I want you to promise me . . ."

"It's no good, Reed, I wouldn't remember what I'd promised. And tomorrow is *Daniel Deronda*. Not to mention my other courses. I hope that letter isn't going to get into the newspapers."

"I think I can promise you that."

"Who do you suppose sent it?" But Reed was already at the door. She waved to him sleepily, ignored the remains of their coffee, and dropped her clothes in a heap on the floor. She was certain she would never get to sleep, with Messenger, Barrister, Emanuel, Sparks, Horan whirling in her mind in that kaleidoscopic way, and was still certain of it when Jerry (for she had forgotten to set the alarm) woke her in the morning.

chapter 13

"IT's A good thing you gave me a key," Jerry said. "I might have gone on ringing, decided you were murdered, lost my head and called in the police. Are you merely hung over?"

"I am *not* hung over, at least not from drink. Get out of here so I can get up. Make some coffee. Do you know how?"

Jerry chortled happily at this question, and left the room. Too late, Kate remembered that he had been a cook in the Army, and that his coffee . . . "Never mind," she called, "I'll make it," But Jerry, who was already running water, did not hear her.

It turned out that Jerry, who gloried in complete ignorance of drip, percolator and filter, had simply dumped some coffee into a saucepan of boiling water; the results were surprisingly good, if one poured with care. Kate, somewhat renovated by her shower and three cups of the brew, cleaned up the shambles of the night before and tried to make up her mind what to do next. Jerry's report of his previous day's activities (considerably edited, and containing no reference to his pursuit of Emanuel) did not seem to make the future course of action any clearer. He ought certainly not to have gone to see Barrister's nurse with that idiotic story; but Kate could not get as exercised over this as she probably should have. It was rapidly being borne in on her that this morning represented a new start. Reed undoubtedly would have insisted that the first step should be to thank Jerry properly and dismiss him. But Kate instinctively knew that when the nebulous plans which were forming in her brain took shape, Jerry would have to be a part of them. There was no one else.

It was eight days since the murder, and already the whole outrageous series of events seemed to be the natural components of Kate's days. She sat down again across the table from Jerry, and thought that here she was, having morning coffee and evolving plots with a young man with whom, in the normal course of events, she would have had nothing whatever to do. Those people who were, two weeks ago, in the forefront of her life had moved somewhere into the background, out of focus. The various issues, literary and otherwise, which had been at the center of her consciousness, now floated vaguely at its periphery. What she sought, of course, was the return to the more orderly world of a fortnight past. Carlyle (to whom she had not given any attention since a week ago yesterday) was supposed to have said, upon hearing that a young lady had decided to accept the universe, "Egad! She'd better!" All Kate asked, she told herself, was to accept, to restore that universe. It had been shattered, but she could not rid herself of the conviction that, with sustained effort and a prayer, it could be put back together again.

"Any new ideas?" Jerry asked.

"I am not lacking ideas," Kate said, "only the ability to make them meaningful. I am beginning to think that Alice was not in Wonderland at all; she was trying to solve a murder. Beautiful suspects keep disappearing, leaving only their grins behind them; others turn into pigs. We are handed a large ungainly bird and asked to play croquet. And running very fast, we are not staying in the same place: we are positively moving backward. A few days ago we had a number of lovely suspects; now all we have is the heir to the murdered girl, and he doesn't have any connection with the case at all. Well, I'd better tell you about him." She recounted the story of Janet Harrison's will, and told him about Messenger's recognition of the picture. (About the letter accusing herself, she said nothing.) Jerry, of course, was elated to hear that the picture was of Barrister, and Kate had wearily to lead him, as she had been led the night before, to the realization that, exciting as the news was, *it* could not be made to lead anywhere.

"The answer must be Messenger. He's probably a very sinister type, with a good front. After all," Jerry continued, "we don't know he wasn't involved with Janet Harrison. We have only his word for it."

"But he denied having heard of her even before he knew she was murdered."

"After he murdered her, you mean."

"Then why identify the picture, and entangle himself further?"

"He didn't entangle himself; he entangled Barrister. Obviously, he never expected to be connected with the whole business at all. He didn't know she'd made a will."

"If he didn't know she'd made a will, why murder her? The motive is supposed to be her money."

"Perhaps it wasn't her money; perhaps it was, but he hoped the will would never be found."

"Jerry, you are getting weakening of the brain. If the will wasn't found, he wouldn't get the money. But, whatever his motive, he wasn't away from Chicago. And don't start suggesting that he hired someone—I simply could not stand discussing that again."

"I don't think this case is helping your disposition—you're beginning to sound petulant. What you need is a vacation."

"What I need is a solution. Keep quiet a minute, and let me think. While it's not a process of which I expect spectacular results, it's the only form of activity that occurs to me at the moment. By the way, if one can make such good coffee by just throwing the ground-up beans in a pot, why are there so many different expensive kinds of coffee makers on the market?"

"Are you asking for my favorite speech on advertising and the distortion of values in America? I do it very well, and have even been known to talk my future in-laws out of the purchase of an ice-crusher, which some clever ad had actually convinced them that they wanted. Perhaps if I were to begin my speech, it would stimulate your thought processes. Ready? Years ago, the objects of a man's desire were clearly divided into two groups: those things he wanted and needed, and those things he wanted simply because they had caught his fancy. It never occurred to this man to confuse the two, or to convince himself that he needed what he merely fancied. The Puritan . . ."

"Can the police possibly *know* that he did not leave Chicago?"

"I've been wondering the same thing," Jerry said. "His colleagues say, Yes, of course Danny boy was working in his laboratory all day; we heard him talking, or rattling test tubes, or using the typewriter, but of course there are records and tapes. Did you see the movie *Laura*? Speaking of records, don't they keep a record of everyone who flies to New York from Chicago?"

"I rather imagine that they do. They have a passenger list for every plane."

"Then he could give a false name, or take the train. I think our next step is to interview Dr. Daniel Messenger. Even if he turns out to be pure as the driven snow, he may tell us something about Barrister, or life, or genes. What can we lose, except the plane fare to Chicago and several days' time?"

"I haven't got several days' time."

"I know; and I haven't got the plane fare to Chicago. I suggest we combine my time and your money, and send me off. I promise not to pull any fancy ones this time; let me get an impression of him."

The idea had already occurred to Kate. She would have dearly loved to talk to Daniel Messenger herself. But if one thing was unarguable, it was that she had to continue in her wonted ways—to be accused of murder is one thing; to abandon one's obligations another. Jerry had more confidence in the value of his impressions than Kate did. This was not precisely personal: as young men went, Jerry had as much sense as could reasonably be expected. The fact was that youngsters cannot judge: she had seen too many half-baked professors popular with students, too many brilliant scholars, a bit on the dull side, scorned. For the student in college there might be a certain rightness in this judgment; but, in this particular instance, Kate was not willing to risk all on the opinion of a twenty-one-year-old who made up in brashness what he lacked in wisdom. Suppose Jerry returned with a definite impression, one way or the other? Would it be worth anything?

Perhaps not. But where was the alternative? Kate vividly remembered arguing once with Emanuel about psychoanalysis as a cure. She had pointed to the length

120

of time it took, its great cost, the lack of control anyone —patient or analyst—had over the process of free association, etcetera, and Emanuel had denied none of it. "It's a very clumsy tool," he had said. "But it's the best we have." Jerry might not be flattered by the analogy, but Kate made it to herself, all the same. A clumsy tool Jerry certainly was, but he was all she had. In any case, apart from Jerry's time and her money, she didn't see what they had to lose—indeed, Jerry, with his frank, youthful masculinity, might well antagonize Messenger less than she.

"The approach, I think," Kate said, "would be to talk to him about Barrister, not about himself. If you're obviously trying to trick him into some dangerous admission, you'll put him off. I know I would be put off. But if you tell him frankly we are in trouble and need his help, you may learn something of value. If he is the murderer, what you learn will not necessarily be worth anything, but then neither would it be if you had a match of wits. Jerry, what I'm saying, bluntly, is that if he's clever enough to have done this, and to have convinced the police of his innocence, you're not going to catch him. On the other hand, if he's as nice as everyone seems to think, he may help us in some way we can't even guess at. Now, I'm not going to let you go out there as Hawkshaw, the great detective, nor do I expect you to pretend to take my advice and then do just what you want." She threw him a piercing glance that made Jerry think of Emanuel and the park. Could she possibly know? In fact, Kate was merely drawing a bow at a venture: she had her suspicions. "Jerry, if you pull any shenanigans this time, that's it. You're back to driving a truck, and no bonus."

"What do I tell Messenger? Who do I say I am?"

"Perhaps we ought to try the truth. Not that I claim any inherent value for it, God forbid; but it has, among our various techniques, the appeal of novelty. Do you need to go home for a suitcase?"

"Well, as a matter of fact . . ." Kate followed Jerry's glance to the foyer; a suitcase stood modestly behind the table.

"Very well, I had better call to see when there is a plane to Chicago." Kate lifted the receiver.

"Eleven-twenty-something. I'll just make it to the airport."

Kate hung up the phone with resignation, and went to get money for Jerry. He was almost out the door before she realized that she had only just told him about Daniel Messenger. How on earth? . . . She got up to ask him.

"The trouble with you," Jerry said, "is that you don't read the newspapers. The police have to give the reporters something, and the contents of the murdered girl's will were just about right. I didn't, of course," he added with becoming modesty, "know about the picture. See you in a few days." He disappeared, closing the door gently behind him, leaving Kate to feel, not for the first time, rather sorry for her niece.

Kate, in her turn, prepared to depart for the university. Reed would undoubtedly have a fit when he learned where Jerry had gone; but the preservation of people's feelings was one of the goods which had vanished with the new state of affairs. Disaster brought ruthlessness in its wake—war had always done so. It was apparently inevitable. She remembered wryly with what difficulty, in the beginning, she had brought herself to use Reed at all. But each ruthless act makes the next one not only possible but inevitable. Perhaps this was how one ended in committing murder.

But what possible series of events, then, had led to this murder? Janet Harrison had had a picture of the young Michael Barrister in her purse, carefully concealed. This seemed certainly to indicate—if one ignored for the moment the possibility of the picture's having been placed there by the murderer—that there was some connection between Barrister and Janet Harrison. Barrister, of course, had denied it. If he had murdered her, carefully concealing the connection between them (perhaps he had searched her room to determine that no evidence of the relationship existed), what was his motive?

Kate left the apartment and went down to wait for a bus. Suppose he had known Janet Harrison when he was a young man, or suppose he had simply known her, and the only picture of him, which, in her infatuation, she could acquire, had been one of him as a young man. In any case, she had got in his hair and he had killed her.

Perhaps she wanted to marry him and he didn't care for her. But surely this was a not uncommon situation; and there are methods of getting rid of importunate young women without killing them, however appealing that solution might appear. Kate had known young women, her own contemporaries, who had become infatuated, had followed the man of their dreams about, spent hours staring up at his bedroom window, telephoned him at outrageous hours of the night. They had appeared desperate enough, yet they were all now married to somebody else, and presumably contented. And if Barrister was the man Janet Harrison had adored, why had she left her money to Messenger, whom she had apparently never seen, whom she certainly had not adored? Or, if it did turn out that she had adored him, why had she carried a picture of Barrister? Jerry suggested that Messenger had put it in her purse, but what would have been the point of that? *No* picture would have been even more confusing than the wrong picture.

Kate arrived at the university in the state of dizziness to which she was becoming fairly accustomed. She sat for a moment in her office, opening her mail in an idle way, and staring at nothing. Her glance fell, inevitably, on the chair where Janet Harrison had sat. "Professor Fansler, do you know a good psychiatrist?" Now, why in the world had the girl asked *her* that question? Was she, Kate, the only older person worthy of respect to whom Janet Harrison had access? It was barely possible. Yet Kate could not help reflecting that the anonymous letter accusing her of the murder had not been as wildly improbable as in her first distress she had thought. Kate stood, somehow, at the center of the enigma. It was she who had sent Janet Harrison to Emanuel; it was there Janet Harrison had been murdered. Had Janet Harrison asked her question of some other professor, for example, she would have ended up, presumably, on some other psychiatrist's couch. Would she have been murdered there? Well, not—Kate forced herself to face this—if Emanuel or Nicola had been the murderer. Otherwise? Well, Barrister had the office across from Emanuel's, and his picture had been recognized by Messenger. Messenger had inherited the money. The farmer takes a wife, the wife takes a child, the child takes a nurse . . . and the cheese stands alone. Who was the cheese?

She was aroused by the telephone from the contemplation of this fascinating question. "Professor Fansler?" Kate admitted it. "This is Miss Lindsay. I'm sorry to disturb you, but you seemed interested enough in the information so that I thought you wouldn't mind. I tried to telephone you at home last night, but there wasn't any answer. I thought you'd rather hear from me than Jackie Miller."

"Yes, of course," Kate said, "it's very nice of you to call. I'm afraid I didn't come away with a very favorable impression of Jackie Miller in her extraordinary pajamas. Are you about to tell me that I am now in her debt?"

"I don't know. But you did seem anxious about the name of the person who had seen Janet Harrison with a man, and the other evening Jackie Miller remembered it. She turned to me and suggested that—um—I might want to tell you what it was." Kate could well imagine what Jackie had said: "You're her pet pigeon, why don't you call her up and tell her?" "Ordinarily," Miss Lindsay went on, "I wouldn't think of bothering you at home, but under the circumstances . . . Of course, as it turned out, I didn't bother you."

"I'm very grateful to you. What's the name? It will all probably turn out to be a mare's nest, but we might as well know."

"Her name is Dribble. Anne Dribble."

"Can anybody possibly be named Dribble?"

"It is unlikely, but that seems to be her name. Jackie thought of it because someone mentioned dribbling. She lived in the dorm here for a short time last semester, but she didn't like it, and moved out soon after. She isn't in the phone book. I'm afraid this isn't very much help."

"On the contrary, I'm very grateful to you. Did you know Miss Dribble at all, well enough, I mean, to decide if she's at all reliable?"

"I didn't know her well, no; barely at all, in fact. But she wasn't—she wasn't Jackie's sort."

"Thank you very much, Miss Lindsay. I expect I can trace her though the university's records. I appreciate your calling." Reed had said that the key to the whole thing might well be here. Probably, however, they would just get another lead that would peter out in some dead end. Kate's class was in fifteen minutes. She called the registrar and requested the address and telephone number of Anne Dribble, who had been registered last semester, possibly this. She was asked to hold on, and did so, not for long. The voice returned to say that Anne Dribble had registered this semester but withdrawn because of illness (this, Kate knew, meant anything from appendicitis to a love affair). Her address was something Waverly Place, and her telephone number . . . Kate wrote it down, and hung up after expressing thanks.

Well, *carpe diem*. She dialed, first for an outside line, then the number. The phone rang at least six times before it was answered by a female clearly aroused from sleep. "May I please speak to Miss Anne Dribble?" Kate asked.

"Speaking." Kate had been certain it would not be this simple. She was going to be late for her lecture.

"Miss Dribble, forgive me for disturbing you, but I think you might be able to help. You know, I'm sure, about the death of Janet Harrison. We have discovered, quite inadvertently, that you saw her in a restaurant some months ago with a man. I wonder if by any chance you know who the man was?"

"Good Lord, I'd forgotten. How in the world . . . ?"

"Miss Dribble, the point is this. Would you recognize that man if you saw him again?"

"Oh, yes, I think so." Kate's heart gave a leap. "They were in a small Czechoslovakian restaurant; I happened to go there because I was visiting a friend who lived down the block from it. Janet Harrison and the man were at the other end, and I had the feeling they didn't want to be approached. But I did look at him. You know, one is curious about the men one's acquaintances go about with, and Janet had always been so mysterious. I think I might recognize him." Kate had not seen Horan; but she thought of Sparks, of Emanuel, of Messenger (who was homely)—could the girl describe the man sufficiently on the phone?

"Miss Dribble, put it this way. If that man were to be lined up with, say, six other men who resembled him superficially, could you pick him out?"

There was a moment's silence. She is going to ask who the hell I am, Kate thought. But all Miss Dribble said

125

was: "I'm not certain. I *think* I would know him again, but I saw him only from a distance in a restaurant. Who . . . ?"

"Miss Dribble, could you give me a quick description of him? Tall, short, fat, thin, dark, fair?" (Emanuel's light hair was now mixed with gray, and looked lighter.) "What sort of person was he?"

"He was sitting down, of course. It's probably quite inaccurate, but if you want a general sort of description, he reminded me of Cary Grant. Good-looking, you know, and suave. I remember being rather surprised that Janet Harrison . . . she was attractive, of course, but this man . . ."

"Thank you, thank you," Kate muttered, hanging up the phone.

Cary Grant!

Yet she managed, just barely, not to be late for the lecture.

chapter 14

"COME into my office," Messenger said. Jerry followed him down the hall with a certain sense of giddiness. This morning he had been talking to Kate; now, a ridiculously short time afterward (though the turning back of his watch accounted somewhat for this), he was about to talk with Messenger, although he had not the slightest idea of what he was going to say. Planning that rigmarole for the nurse had been one thing, his fumbling with Horan another, but Messenger made both of these techniques impossible. Jerry could not have named the particular quality that marked Messenger, though he recognized it. Nature had bestowed on Messenger none of her usual frivolous endowments; he had neither looks, nor any sort of physical grace, nor wit, nor superficial cleverness. He was simply himself. Jerry was to try later to explain it to Kate, with no great success. All he could think of to say was that Messenger was *there*. Most people were a collection of mannerisms, but they were not simply *there*, themselves. In any case, Kate's instinct had been right: only the truth was possible.

Jerry explained, therefore, about Emanuel and Kate, about himself and the job he had taken, about the trucks he had driven before and the law school he was planning to attend. "We've come to you for help," Jerry said, "because you seem the one person who might possibly connect some of the odd bits and pieces that we have. Janet Harrison left you her money—that connects you with her, even if she was unknown to you. And you knew Barrister. So far, no two people in this mess connect at all, except, of course, Kate and Emanuel, and neither of them killed Janet Harrison. Perhaps, if you were to tell me something about Barrister . . ."

127

"I'm afraid the only things I could tell you about him would not be precisely useful to your purpose, which I gather is to cast Mike in the role of chief murderer. Of course, he's probably changed somewhat; most people do. I wouldn't have guessed that Mike would end up with a practice among rich ailing women, but I'm not surprised now that I know it. It's very easy for doctors to make a great deal of money today, and most of them do. I don't mean doctors are more moneygrubbing than anybody else—there are too few doctors, and many opportunites to get rich. And most doctors feel," Messenger smiled, "that they are owed some return for what is an immensely long and expensive training. One of my young daughters thinks now she would like to be a doctor, and I've figured out that it would cost about $32,000 to make her one. All that this means is that the Barrister you are investigating isn't quite the same as the Mike I knew—and I never knew him all that well. He was a reticent sort of person."

"You're not rich." This was not, Jerry realized, to the point, but Messenger interested him.

"No, nor noble either. I don't happen to be interested in most of the things that are expensive, and I'm married to a woman who finds making do a fascinating challenge. She likes to plan, to make clothes, to do things—in the old way. And she likes to have a job. I think that the work I'm doing is the most interesting, important work there is; and, to be frank, I feel sorry for everybody who isn't doing it. But I don't do it because it doesn't pay all that much. I'd be doing the same thing even if it happened that doing this made me rich as Croesus."

"Was Mike like that, when you knew him?"

"Who can tell? I've found that young men have ideas, and theories, but you never know what you are until you become it. Do you read C. P. Snow?" Jerry shook his head. "Interesting writer, to me, anyway; I don't know if your Professor Fansler would agree. In one of his books, he has his narrator say that there's only one test for discovering what you really want: it consists in what you have. But Mike was too young then to make the test; you're too young now.

"I will say this," Messenger continued, "though I'm afraid it won't help you very much—quite the contrary. Mike wasn't the sort who could kill anyone. Not possibly, in my opinion. To carry out a murder requires at least two qualities of personality, I should think. One is what we might call a streak of sadism, for lack of a better word, and the other is the ability to concentrate on what one wants to the exclusion of everything else. To see people, not as people, but as obstacles to be removed."

"You mean he loved people, and animals, and couldn't bear to see anyone hurt?"

Messenger smiled. "That sounds sentimental. Anyone who wants to be a doctor knows that people have to be hurt, that people suffer. People who never cause pain never cause anything else; and Mike wanted then, at least, to cause a good deal. I don't remember what he felt about animals—certainly he never had one when I knew him. What I mean sounds overblown when you put it into words: he never caused pain for the hell of it—you know, by a triumph of wit or a clever joke. And he never withheld kindness. I don't read poetry, but I had to listen to some in college courses; and I always remember one line which seemed to me very well to describe much of life today, perhaps always: 'greetings where no kindness is.' Mike didn't go in for that sort of greeting. But you mustn't think I'm describing a saint. Mike was very good-looking and attractive to women. He had a good time."

Jerry looked depressed. It seemed horrible that their chief suspect should turn out to be incapable of murder. But that, after all, was Messenger's opinion, and was Messenger all that smart? He, Jerry, had in college (just to take one instance) been party to a joke that involved an awkward, rather effeminate young man and an exceedingly slick and experienced young woman. He remembered it still with something remarkably close to pleasure. And certainly kindness was nothing to which he had given much thought—and as for this garbage about greetings. . . . Yet he was not capable of murder either. Not even if . . . well, one never really knew; that's what it came down to. If one knew, there would be fewer unsolved murders.

Messenger seemed to read his thoughts. "I'm no authority, you know, no student of human nature. Just my impressions."

"You shared a room when you were residents, you and Barrister. Did you know him before?"

"No. The hospital helped you find rooms, and roommates. When we were on duty, of course, we slept at the hospital, so home was really where we slept when we got the chance, and kept beer in a secondhand icebox."

"Did you ever meet Barrister's family?"

"He didn't have any, to speak of. Surely the police found out all about that. In fact, the detective who came to see me mentioned it. Mike was an orphan, as he was fond of saying, with a grin. He'd been the only child of an only child, and was brought up by his grandparents; they were both dead when I knew him. I gather he had a happy childhood. You know, I remember something he said once about Lawrence, the writer, I mean. Mike was a great reader."

"Literature seems to be following me around in this case."

"Odd, isn't it? I've already quoted poetry and Snow, and I don't think I've been guilty of a literary reference in years. Perhaps it's the influence of your Professor Fansler. I don't know why I should think of books in connection with Mike. But the only specific thing he ever told me about his childhood had to do with D. H. Lawrence."

"Lady Chatterley's Lover?" Jerry asked.

"I don't think so; were there any children in that?"

"No," Jerry said. "Not born yet, anyway."

"Well, it wasn't that then. In this book there was a little girl, frightened for some reason, and her stepfather carried her about with him while he fed the cows. I don't really know what the connection is, because Mike's grandfather didn't have cows. But something about the way his grandfather comforted him, after his parents were killed—Lawrence had caught that, Mike said. It doesn't sound very important. I don't know why I mention it. Anyway, Mike didn't have much family, though there was some old lady he used to write to."

"Did he have any special woman then?"

"Not that I know of. You're thinking, perhaps, Janet Harrison knew him then, and I didn't know about it. Well, it's not impossible, I suppose. Mike didn't talk about his women, but surely the police know where Janet Harrison was at that time."

"Did he go away much?"

"No. When we had short vacations we slept."

"How long were you together?"

"A year, more or less. For the length of our residency. I came to Chicago. Mike thought he might, too, but he didn't."

"Where did he go?"

"New York. You know that."

"Did you hear from him in New York?"

"No. I don't think he went there right away. He went on a vacation first, camping. We both like camping. I was supposed to go with him, but then, at the last minute, I couldn't. He went on up to Canada—I had a card from him. I told all this to the detective. That's the last I heard of him, except for Christmas cards. We exchanged those for a few years, later on."

"It seems odd you never saw him in New York."

"I've only been there a few times, for medical conventions. I took the family, and any spare time I had I spent with them. Once I saw Mike, but we didn't really have time to get together. Anyway, there wouldn't have been very much point to it."

"It's all clear enough, I guess, except why she left you the money. You didn't save her life once, and forget about it?"

"I don't save lives. I can't, of course, say positively that I never laid eyes on her, but I don't think I did, and certainly not for any length of time. It just doesn't make any sense at all. You don't really know, do you, that Mike ever knew her? So the fact that I once knew Mike isn't really all that conclusive. I'd like to help you; I just can't think of any way I can."

"Are you going to take the money? Perhaps I haven't any business asking you that."

"It's a natural enough question. I don't know that I'll get the money. The girl was murdered, and she has some family who might, I suppose, contest the will. But if I got the money I would take it, provided there was no one with a real claim. I could use the money—couldn't anyone? Besides, there's something odd about a windfall—one never expected it, and then, when one hears of it, one is convinced it was somehow deserved."

"Did Mike know you were going into research?"

"Oh, yes, everyone knew that. Mike used to say if I was going to live the rest of my life on four thousand a year—that's what they paid in those days—I'd better marry a rich wife or one who liked to work. I took his advice, you see—the latter part of it."

Jerry could have spun out the questions—there were many that occurred to him, but he could guess most of the answers, and didn't think them very important, in any case. Messenger could, of course, have been lying. He could have been in league with Barrister for years. But even if they could have concocted this murder for $25,000 between them, Messenger didn't look capable of it. His honesty was so patent that it was, Jerry thought, impossible to be in his presence and even consider the idea of his involvement in a plot. He might be shrewd enough, but he seemed one of those rare persons who say what they mean, and mean what they say—surely the wrong sort to plan some diabolical scheme. Jerry stood up.

"There was one other thing," he said, "though I don't really have to bother you with it. You'll just save me some research. In law, you have to pass the bar exam of the state in which you intend to practice. That's true in the East. There's a certain reciprocity, of course, but if you practice in New York, you have to have passed the New York bar exam. If you've taken the New Jersey bar exam, that won't do. Isn't the same thing true in medicine? Did Barrister have to take the New York exam in order to practice there?"

"No. There's something called the National Board of Medical Examiners—they give a certificate which is accepted as adequate qualification by almost all the states. There are some exceptions, I don't remember what they are, but New York isn't one of them. Other states require some sort of oral or written examination. But Mike had no more exams to take in order to practice in New York—probably he had to register, or something of the sort."

"Thank you, Dr. Messenger. You've been very kind."

"Not much help, I'm afraid. Let me know if anything else occurs to you. I think you'll find, you know, that Mike didn't do it. People leave tastes behind them; Mike didn't leave that kind of taste." He bowed Jerry out. Jerry, going back to the hotel to put in a long-distance call to Kate, felt that Messenger left a fine taste, no doubt of that; but the case as a whole had by now a taste that could be described only as rancid.

chapter 15

KATE rushed away from the lecture room, leaving behind her the students who had come up to ask questions, and ignoring, outside her office, the students gathered there. She put in a call to Reed.

"I've found a Miss Dribble—you know, the one who talked to Jackie-wackie when there was soap in the fountain. She says he looks like Cary Grant. Is it all right to talk now?"

"My dear girl, if we are being overheard, I hope the eavesdropper understands you better than I. Shall we risk a little more clarity? Who dribbled?"

"That's her name. Dribble. Anne Dribble. Remember, you said she would hold the key to the whole thing?"

"I don't remember ever mentioning anyone of that name in my life. Is she someone who knew Janet Harrison? If so, she will go down in history, though it's a pity to immortalize a name like that."

"She knew Janet Harrison slightly; she used to live in the dorm—Dribble, I mean. Jackie Miller remembered that she, still Dribble, was the one who had told her, Jackie, that she had seen her, Janet, with a man. Apparently someone dribbled at breakfast, which reminded Jackie —there are advantages to having a verb for a name— who it was who had spoken to her of seeing Janet with a man; and she, Jackie, told her, Miss Lindsay; and she, Miss Lindsay, called me, Kate. I called her, Miss Dribble, and she said she *thought* she would recognize the man again, but if I wanted a quick description he looked like Cary Grant, good-looking and suave. You have twenty minutes; rewrite that into an acceptable English sentence."

"Kate, I know we need suspects, but do you really

think Cary Grant is likely to have killed her? I could, of course, call Hollywood . . ."

"Reed—which of our suspects looks like Cary Grant?"

"You forget, I haven't seen any of our suspects."

"You mentioned yourself that the young man in the picture looked like Cary Grant."

"Did I?"

"Yes. And Barrister still does, in a general sort of way. I mean, he's older, but so is Cary Grant."

"And so am I. Getting older by the minute. What do you want me to do, offer Barrister a part in pictures?"

"Got it in one. I want some pictures. I want to show them to Miss Dribble, and if she recognizes Barrister, we've got proof, actual proof, that Barrister knew her. Of course, it *may* be Sparks or Horan. Emanuel looks nothing like Cary Grant."

"Believe it or not, I begin to get your drift. Look, I'll suggest to them at Homicide that Barrister looks like Cary Grant. I'll probably be recommended for the vacation I so badly need. Have you got Miss Dribble's address?"

Kate gave it to him. "And, Kate," Reed went on, "don't mention Miss Dribble or her address to anyone else, there's a good girl."

"Reed! You *do* think there may be something in it."

"I'll call you at home this evening. Go home and stay there. I mean it; that's an order. Don't go dashing off following clues. Promise?"

"Is it all right with you if I hold my office hours and meet my afternoon class?"

"Go home the minute the class is over. Stay home. Neither walk nor run to the nearest exit. Sit. You'll hear from me." And with this Kate had to be content.

Following the afternoon class, Kate returned to her office to find the phone ringing. It was Emanuel.

"Kate, can I see you for a few minutes?" he asked.

"Has anything happened?"

"That's what I want to talk to you about. Where can we meet for a cup of coffee?"

"How about Schrafft's? It's a good place for convincing oneself that life goes on."

"Very well, then, Schrafft's in twenty minutes."

But both of them got there in fifteen. The place was

135

quiet, except for a few ladies noisily consuming their afternoon calories at the counter.

"Kate," Emanuel said, "I'm beginning to worry."

"Don't begin now. If they'd had enough evidence, they'd have pulled you in as a material witness. I think it's going to be all right, if we just hold on a little longer."

"Where did you learn to talk like that? You sound like one of those authentic precinct novels. It's not me I'm worried about; it's you. I had to go down to see them again today, both Nicola and I did, but it was you they wanted to talk about. In the old days," he added, as the waitress approached, "you used to eat ice cream covered with gooey fudge and nuts. Do you want that now?"

"Just coffee." Emanuel gave the order to the waitress. "Look, Emanuel, I'll tell you this, but I'm not supposed to know it, and you're not supposed to know it, so don't mention it to the police or Nicola. They've got an anonymous letter accusing me. I'm supposed to have murdered her because I'm in love with you and jealous of Nicola. The police have to follow it up. After all, if it turned out in the end I'd done it, they'd look pretty silly if they hadn't followed up a lead like that. And to give them their due, I'm not a bad suspect, as I think I pointed out before."

"This has happened because you tried to help me."

"This has happened because I sent you the girl who was murdered. Emanuel, I've been wondering, why did she come to me for the name of a psychiatrist? I can't help feeling that there's something important about the fact that she did."

"I've been over and over that fact in my mind. But after all, she had to ask someone. You'd be surprised at the abandon with which most people pick a psychiatrist—never bothering to discover if he's properly qualified, a doctor, or anything else. To ask an intelligent, educated person for the name of a psychiatrist is not the worst way to go about finding one."

"But you're thinking that if you'd never backed onto the Merritt Parkway none of this would have happened."

"That's nonsense. The one thing a psychiatrist knows is that things don't 'happen.' "

"Oh, yes, I'd forgotten. If you break your leg it means you wanted to, deep down."

136

"What's worrying me, Kate, is that the detective's questions about you disturbed me, and I talked a lot more than I've talked up to now. I've been rather reticent about my patients, but I wasn't reticent about you. I tried to explain our relationship. I told them, if they wanted a psychiatrist's opinion, you were incapable of murder, and incapable of stealing pieces on Henry James. I realize now, somewhat too late, that they have probably mistaken my vehemence for personal passion, and will now decide that we planned it together."

"And if we are seen here, they will be certain we are now plotting further."

Emanuel looked horrified. "I hadn't thought of that. I only wanted to . . ."

"It was a joke, Emanuel. When I first heard they were accusing me, I was terrified, with the feeling of panic a small child has when he's lost his parents in a crowd. But I don't feel that way anymore. I didn't do it, and the evidence that I did is nonsense. Actually, I think we may be getting near the end of this horror. I have that feeling of events closing in. But I don't want to say any more yet, in case it doesn't work out."

"Kate. Don't get into trouble."

"At least you'll know that if I do, my inner psyche willed it. That's another joke. Try to smile."

"Nicola's beginning to feel the strain. For a while her natural exuberance kept her afloat, but now she's beginning to sink. And my patients are starting to wonder. If I didn't do it, it seems odd that they can't find the person who did. I feel frightened, genuinely frightened, in a small-boy way. Why can't they look elsewhere? Why do they keep walking round and round us?"

"The police have you, or you and Nicola, or you and me, and that's the case they're trying to prove. To them, the fact that it happened on your couch is a nice, simple, unassailable fact. You can't expect them to look around for evidence that they're wrong. But if we put the evidence right under their noses, they'll have to look at it. That's what I'm trying to do, in my wild and woolly way. Instead of worrying, why don't you try to think of something Janet Harrison said?"

"Freud was interested in puns."

"Was he? I've always agreed with the estimation of them

137

as the lowest form of wit. I remember once, when I was a child, saying 'I'm thirsty,' and some odious friend of my father's said, 'I'm Joe.' Or isn't that a pun?"

"Janet Harrison had, twice, a disturbing dream about a man who was a lawyer."

"A lawyer. The one thing we don't have in this case is a lawyer. Didn't she have any other dreams? Perhaps the lawyer who made her will . . ."

"You see, the censor works even when you dream. It won't present a thought too disturbing, perhaps because you might wake, or because the unconscious won't let it through."

"Oh, yes, Brooks Brothers, and the awful suit. Sorry, go on."

"We pun in our dreams, as well as when we're awake. Sometimes in several languages."

"Sounds like Joyce."

"Very like Joyce. He understood all about it. I'm wondering if Janet Harrison didn't pun in her dream, not in another language, but in the same language, an ocean away. What a lawyer, in England?"

"They've got two kinds—solicitors and . . . Emanuel! Barrister again!"

"I wondered. Of course, she may just have seen his name outside his door across the hall from me. As evidence, it's worth nothing to a policeman and very little to a psychiatrist, at least by itself. He may just have looked like her father, or someone else; dreams are very involved, and there isn't often a one-to-one relation . . ."

"I think she knew him, I'm sure she did, and before too long I'll prove it. Emanuel, I love you. I hope no policeman can hear me."

"You realize, of course, that Messenger's name is also capable of lots of . . ."

"What did she feel about the lawyer, in her dream?"

"I've looked up my notes: fear, mainly. Fear, and hate."

"Not love?"

"That's very hard to distinguish from hate in a dream, and frequently in life. But speaking of patients' dreams, I'd better get back to the next set."

"She never mentioned Cary Grant, did she?"

"No. Kate, you will be careful, won't you?"

"Psychiatrists are so illogical. They tell you nothing

happens by accident, and then they tell you to be careful. No, don't drive me home. It will make you late, and God knows what it would suggest to a lurking detective, if any."

It was Kate's day for walking in on ringing phones. The one in her apartment had the angry sound of a phone that has been ringing for a long time.

"Miss Kate Fansler, please."

"Speaking."

"Chicago calling. One moment, please. Go ahead, please. Here is your party."

"Well, I've seen him," Jerry said, "and I'm afraid we've wasted your money; my time isn't worth much. My impression, for what it's worth, is that he didn't do it. His impression, for what it's worth, is that Barrister didn't do it. Our conversation was full of literary allusions— your influence, he seemed to think—perhaps they are right about E.S.P. Who said 'greetings where no kindness is'?"

"Wordsworth."

"Kate, you should have gone on one of those quiz shows."

"Nope. They wanted me to split with the director, and I refused."

"Do you want me to tell you what he said? It's your money."

"No, don't tell me—write it down. Get down every bit of it you can remember. Somewhere, somehow, there's one little straw of a fact that is going to break the back of this case, and it may be in that interview of yours. All right, I admit it's unlikely; but, as you said, it's my money and your time isn't worth much. Write it all down."

"On little pieces of hotel stationery?"

"Jerry, you must not allow yourself to get discouraged. What did you expect, that Messenger would lock the door and tell you with a glint in his eye that he'd killed Janet Harrison long distance by means of a secret ray gun he'd just developed? We're going to find the answer to this case, but I think the answer will first appear on the horizon as a cloud no bigger than a man's hand. Get the interview written down—rent a typewriter, find a public stenographer, scribble it out on hotel stationery and then get it copied—I don't care. But come home on the first plane you can get out of Chicago. I'll see you in the morning."

Barrister had known Janet Harrison—of this Kate was now convinced. That he had the office across from Emanuel's might be the wildest of coincidences, but it could not be coincidence that he had once known the man to whom Janet Harrison had left her money; it could not be coincidence that he was seen in a restaurant (and Kate was certain he had been) with Janet Harrison; it could not be a coincidence that Janet Harrison had punned so cleverly in her dreams—though she would hate to have to convince Reed, let alone a court of law, of this last one.

Had they met in New York? There was, of course, no evidence at all of this, but the chances were certainly that they had. Probably Barrister had mentioned Messenger, never knowing that Janet Harrison would indulge in the quixotic gesture of making out a will in his favor. Kate didn't remember now where Barrister had come from, but she was fairly certain it was not Michigan—and, of a sudden, something began to root about at the base of Kate's mind. A small disturbing noise it made, like the sound of a mouse behind the wainscoting.

Whatever it was, it evaded her. But wait—if Janet Harrison had met Barrister in New York, she must have met him very soon after his arrival, for the picture she carried was of a younger man. Perhaps it was the only picture Barrister had—perhaps she had stolen it. But why had she hidden it so carefully inside her driver's license? Well, say she had stolen it. I must *not*, Kate thought, starting going round and round again. Let's stick to the one thing I've established—well, established at any rate to my own satisfaction: Barrister knew Janet Harrison. Of course, they would have to confront the Dribble girl with him, but she, Kate, had no doubts of the result of this.

Kate began to make herself supper, wondering when Reed would call. No doubt he would point out that, as a detective, Kate made an excellent literary critic. Although Reed had always been too polite to say so, at least in so many words, Kate knew he thought of literary critics as operating in a rarefied atmosphere far removed from earthly facts. Highbrow critics, he would probably say . . . again Kate was aware of the mouse behind the wainscoting. That same mental disturbance she had just felt when she had thought of . . . what? Of where Barrister had come from.

What had he said then, that day in Nicola's apartment? "Aren't you from New York?" Kate had asked him. And he had answered that, as some highbrow critic had said, he was a young man from the provinces. Some highbrow critic who had talked about a certain kind of novel. Well, that highbrow critic had a name: Trilling. But did Barrister know it? Did Barrister read the *Partisan Review,* or a collection of essays called *The Opposing Self?* It was not impossible—yet his tone of voice had been that of one who scorns these matters. Where had he heard Trilling's phrase for a certain kind of novel?

He had heard it from her, Kate Fansler, by way of Kate's student, Janet Harrison. Not a doubt in the world. Again, it was not the kind of evidence of which any policeman could be persuaded to take official notice, but to Kate it was unquestionable. Janet Harrison had listened to that phrase used by Kate, had been struck with it, and had repeated it to Barrister. That meant not only that Barrister had known Janet Harrison, but that he had known her (it seemed likely) when she had still been taking a course of Kate's. So Barrister was a young man from the provinces, was he? Well, one thing that marked the young man from the provinces, in literature at least, had been that he, or someone he had been associated with, had always come to what an English friend of Kate's called a "sticky end." A young man from the provinces indeed!

When Reed called, Kate was ready for him.

"I've got quite a bit to report," Reed said. "I'll be up to see you in a few hours. Is that too late?"

"No. But, Reed, you might as well be prepared—I'm convinced of one thing anyway. And you needn't laugh uproariously. Barrister knew Janet Harrison."

"I'm not laughing," Reed said. "That's one of the things I'm coming to tell you. He's just admitted it."

chapter 16

"IT'S A funny thing about the uncon-
scious mind," Kate said to Reed some hours later. "There
was no real reason for Barrister to use that phrase about the
young man from the provinces when talking to me—I'm
certain he had no idea why it came into his head. But he
met me, realized who I was, knew about me because Janet
Harrison had told him about me, knew he must not on any
account reveal that he knew about me, and his unconscious came up with the young man from the provinces."

"Observant chap, Freud. He made a number of sug-
gestions about word tests for suspected criminals—
did you know? It's more or less the principle a lie
detector works on, or is supposed to work on: the criminal's blood pressure increases when he's faced with a
disturbing idea. In Freud's test, he blocks at the disturbing question, or associates in a telling way. Anyhow, Barrister, like a good patient on the couch, decided this afternoon to talk to the point. It's amazing how frightened
innocent people can get when faced with investigation."

"Are liars innocent—I mean people who lie about important things that entangle other people in meshes of
untruth?"

"The truth's a slippery thing. Perhaps that's why only
literary people understand it."

"That's what Emanuel would call a provocative remark."

"And he'd be right. I apologize. Except, of course,
that the remark is true. You'd figured out Barrister had
known her before we did. And your discovery of Miss
Dribble urged me to urge them to put on the pressure
sooner than they might have. It was Miss Dribble (since
I did not yet know about the young man from the provinces) which encouraged me to go along for the interview,

142

even though I had no official right to do any such thing."

"What did he say? Father, I cannot tell a lie, especially when it looks as though I may be found out?"

"He was quite frank about the whole thing. He didn't think anyone knew they knew each other; and, what with his little trouble about the malpractice suit, he didn't like to risk being entangled with the police. You have to admit he wasn't in an enviable position, the girl killed next door, and he having known her. He quite simply hoped we'd never find out there was any connection between them; and, in fact, if it hadn't been for the will and the picture, we probably never would have. And Miss Dribble, of course."

"Of course. Someone was bound to have seen them, one time or another. If the police had investigated him more, and Emanuel less, they might have found someone else who had seen them by now. Didn't the fact that Miss Dribble had been dug up by me, another suspect, make them suspicious about that evidence?"

"You've more or less been demoted from the list of suspects—the active list, anyway. They did quite a little investigation of you, as you will doubtless be hearing from your friends and associates. Your colleagues considered the idea that you would steal a piece of work from a student ridiculous, and they went on to point out, with some heat, I understand, the various complications of scholarly research. Also—please try not to get upset—the idea that you were still in love with Emanuel, if you ever had been, was proved untenable by the fact that you had been, more recently, in love with someone else."

"I see. Did they discover his name?"

"Oh, yes, they saw him. Kate, this is a murder case. I'm sorry to have to mention it—but I'd rather you heard about it first from me, and were prepared. You're not, I understand, at the moment planning to marry? Sorry— I shouldn't have asked that. Anyway, there didn't seem much reason why you should have done it, and, of course, there were other things apart from motive which made you unlikely. You aren't angry, are you?"

"No, not angry, and not planning to be married. Now, don't get all nervous and fumble with your dispatch case. I appreciate your honesty, and I want to hear more about

Barrister. What did he say, exactly? Had they been having a grand passion?"

"He met her at about the time the picture was taken—he needed it for some official reason or other. I think he would have liked to be vague about when he knew her, but we've had a man working on Janet Harrison's history —you *do* underestimate the forces of law, my dear—and he discovered that Janet Harrison had gone on an extended trip to the wilds of Canada. I guess Barrister knew that we would soon discover, if we hadn't—and as a matter of fact we hadn't—that he too had been in the same wilds, so he told us they were together there. I gather it was one of those romances, as with people who meet on a cruise or in Italy, lifted out of the daily round of life and unlikely to endure after the return to the daily round. After that Barrister came to New York, and as far as he was concerned it was finished, at least as a serious attachment. But Janet Harrison decided to become a nurse, apparently the better to be a doctor's wife, and then she had to go home when her mother died. After one thing and another, and the passage of years, even though she hadn't heard from him especially, she came to New York. She needed some sort of excuse, so she decided to study English literature at your university. We don't know why she picked that over history, which had been her college major."

"I can guess at one possible reason, though she may just have thought it was easier to read novels than learn dates. The history department demands that its applicants take something called a Graduate Record Exam; the English department doesn't. Therefore she would have less trouble getting accepted by the graduate English department —her college record would do it."

"You're probably right. At any rate, there she was. She was naturally a most unconfiding sort, he says—which God knows we've discovered—and he managed to keep the relationship quiet and to see her only occasionally, though she *was* a nuisance. He admits it. Apparently she decided to go to an analyst in order to get over her infatuation, though Barrister didn't call it that, and the fact that she hit on Emanuel was coincidence—though Barrister did know that she admired you very much, which is why she asked you to recommend someone. He hoped she'd be cured, and even offered, he told us, to help pay the fees.

He was very frank, Kate, and, I'm afraid, very believable. Like you, he underestimates the police, and thought, if they had a nice motive like that, he'd be for it. The shock when Nicola called him in to look at the body was considerable—I can well believe it. It's to his credit that he called the police immediately. Incidentally, he could have said he had to examine her, shut the door, and looked through her bag, in which case he might have found that picture. He did no such thing."

"That picture must have given him a jolt."

"No question that the police slipped up there. But of course they thought it was a recent photograph, so I suppose they are to be forgiven. As I say, he told all this quite openly, throwing himself on the mercy of the police. He admitted he was telling it now because the police seemed close to finding it out. He also said that men don't kill women who are inconveniently in love with them, and he hoped we realized it."

"Were they lovers?"

"He was asked that, although the police call it having an intimate relationship. He hesitated over that one—that is, he said 'no' at first, and then said they had been, in the wilds of Canada. He smiled and said he supposed she might have told Emanuel that, so he'd better admit it; he was younger, etcetera, etcetera, but he was emphatic that they had not been 'intimate' in New York. He said openly he had not the slightest intention of marrying her, and to have made love to her would have made him both a cad and a fool. A fool, because what he wanted was for her to go quietly away."

"What about Messenger?"

"He admitted that puzzled him. He *had* spoken to her about Messenger, in Canada, with great admiration apparently, but why she should make a will leaving her money to Messenger years later Barrister didn't know. Messenger is going to have to bear a certain amount of looking into, there's no question of that."

"And Barrister didn't steal the porter's uniform and burgle her room?"

"The police asked him about that, in a roundabout way. He threw up his hands and said that if he would lie to the police in order to avoid a scandal, he was certainly not, as a women's doctor, going to get himself caught wandering around a women's dormitory. He admitted to being relieved as hell that she lived there, since it meant he didn't have to make excuses for not going to her room, and there's no question he avoided the place like the plague."

"It's still odd their relationship was so secret."

"I know that, and so does he. It's one of the things that puts him on the spot. But, Kate, you'd be amazed the queer things that turn up in people's lives, once you start rooting around. I could many a tale unfold. And when the police start asking questions because someone's been connected with a murder case, at least half the time that someone has something he isn't too proud of, or doesn't want known, and he'll lie and muck up the investigation. For example, Nicola once got fed up enough with her husband to fling off and have an affair with another man—did you know that?"

"No."

"All right, and remember, you don't know it now. Nicola didn't tell us, nor Emanuel. We found it out. Well, Barrister is found out, too. But while it sounds illogical, because he did try to keep the relationship secret after the murder, he still would not necessarily, or even probably, have figured that he could keep it quiet if he were deciding to murder her, at least the way I see it. And the motive just won't do. If you think about it calmly, you'll admit it."

"I've already admitted it, damn it!"

"When there's a murder, the police lift up a rock that's been in place a long time. And if you've ever lifted up such a rock, you know that there are all sorts of slimy, crawly things underneath. Human beings, by and large, are not a very commendable lot."

"So we're back with Emanuel?"

"They haven't been able to prove that Emanuel ever saw Janet Harrison outside of the office, but then you see how long they took to establish the connection with Barrister."

"How many men was she supposed to have been seeing, in her quiet way?"

"You never know, with that type. If the police could get one outside witness, one piece of corroborating evidence, I'd think they'd risk an arrest. Of course, the District Attorney's office is not happy to see arrests if they think they'll lose the case when it comes to trial."

"But the way I've heard it, they'll push the case if they've got enough evidence, even when they know in their heart of hearts that the accused is innocent."

"Sometimes. But the police don't have hearts of hearts. They don't work on flair. They work on evidence; the more circumstantial, the better. As it is, between you and me, I think they might risk it with Emanuel. It was *his* couch, *his* knife, *his* patient, and he was the only one likely to be sitting in his chair, with her lying down. There have been cases with no more evidence than that. But his office was, so to speak, wide open, of which a good defense lawyer could make plenty. If they can establish motive, they've got him, though."

"Is that what you think will happen, Reed?"

"No. I believe you, and I believe your judgment of him. But, Kate, where else are we going to look? The police don't think it's likely that a homicidal maniac was at work, and I agree with them. Of course, Messenger's a possibility, but an awfully farfetched one."

"Why can't they arrest Barrister as well as Emanuel? Barrister had the motive. I know it's not the world's greatest motive, but, speaking of smart lawyers . . ."

"The motive without the evidence isn't enough. Anyway, not a motive like that. Well, at least things are breaking. At least we've got the detectives started on Sparks and Horan, and something may come from there. What, by the way, has happened to your Jerry?"

"I sent him out to see Messenger."

"Kate, I really think, after what I said . . ."

"I know—rave on. If Jerry comes up with any startling facts, I promise to tell you. But judging from his report over the phone, Messenger is another innocent babe. You know, Reed, it would be a hell of a blow to psychiatry if they arrested Emanuel. I mean, he's not a fly-by-night crank, or someone who had just taken up psychiatry. He's a member of, and therefore backed by, the most austere institute of psychiatry in the country. Even I, who argue with Emanuel constantly, cannot believe that they would admit as a member, after the extended analysis they require, a man who could murder a patient on a couch. And I'm sure they didn't. Even if he weren't convicted, his arrest would be a hell of a blow. Perhaps there's someone around who loathes psychiatry, and he's going to murder patients at regular, widely spaced intervals, in order to discredit the profession. Maybe you'd better ask all the suspects what they think about psychiatry."

"I'll make a note of it. Now I must go and get some sleep. *I've* got a trial coming up tomorrow—grand jury, question of pornography. Perhaps we ought to blow ourselves up, all of us, and start again, after the earth has cooled a few hundred years, and try to make a better job of it."

With which happy thought, Kate went to bed.

In the morning Jerry, looking downcast, arrived with his report. He sat angrily flipping the pages of a magazine while Kate read his notes. Jerry had reported his conversation with Messenger in the form of dialogue; this was followed by an exact, unflattering description of the doctor and completed by an account of Jerry's impressions. He might not have felt there was much substance in the report, but he had taken care with its form. Kate congratulated him on his neatness, but he sneered.

"You *were* literary," she said.

"Weren't we, though? Do you recognize that thing from Lawrence he was gabbing on about?"

"Oh, yes, I think so. It must have made quite an impression on Barrister. It's from the beginning of *The Rainbow*—nobody ever did children better than Lawrence, which is probably because he didn't have any. I take it Messenger was a man you would have felt inclined to trust."

"Yes, he was, if that's worth anything. I'm sure it isn't. In fact, if you want to know, he reminded me of you."

"Of me? Do my ears stick out?"

Jerry flushed. "I didn't mean physically. The impression I have of him was like the impression I have of you. Don't ask me what I mean—it's just that, both of you might be dishonest, but you'd know you were doing it."

"That's a nice compliment, Jerry."

"Is it? It's probably pure, unadulterated crap. What do I do now?"

"He didn't give the impression that he was being dishonest and knowing it?"

"No, he didn't. I'd swear he was honest. Yet people will swear that confidence men are honest."

"I think," Kate said, "that we'll assume he's honest. At least until we have any reason to doubt it. There has to be a constant in every equation—up to now we've had only variables. I think we'll put Messenger in as the constant, and then see what X turns out to equal. Jerry, would you mind awfully much just hanging around? I *think* I may send you to Michigan. The trouble is, if you want to know, we have been approaching this whole problem with fettered imaginations."

She began to pace up and down the room. Jerry groaned.

chapter 17

IT HAD been Thursday morning when Kate had spoken to Jerry. It was now Friday evening. Kate had that day again asked someone to take her lectures. She faced Reed, who sat on her couch, his legs stretched out before him.

"I don't know if I can tell you what happened, properly, from the beginning," she said, "but I can tell you where I began yesterday morning. I began with an idle joke, from one doctor to another, months ago. I began with a dated photograph. I began with one of the great modern novels, and a scene in it, indelibly impressed on the mind of a man because it recalled to him a vital moment of his childhood. I began with a punning association in a dream, an association not of love or infatuation, but hate or fear. I began also with an old lady, and the wilds of Canada.

"I had decided to believe Messenger—you read Jerry's report just now. Messenger said Barrister wasn't capable of murder, and while that statement might be doubted, I decided not, for the moment, to doubt it.

"There were a few other facts whirling around also. A suit for malpractice. Sparks, who never forgets a face. Nicola, and her willingness to tell a sympathetic listener, or even an unsympathetic one, almost anything he may want to know about her life. A window cleaner, who turned out never to exist, but who suggested to me the ease with which anyone, with access to the court outside Emanuel's office and kitchen, could study those rooms. My visits to see Emanuel and Nicola, in the good old days before the crime. A question put to me, 'Professor Fansler, do you know a good psychiatrist?'

"These were all whirling around, as I say, but suddenly

on Thursday morning they seemed to fall into place. I then did, or caused to be done, three things.

"The first involved Nicola. I called her up, and urged her to get herself, as subtly as possible, into a conversation with Barrister. This wasn't hard for Nicola. She simply appeared at his office door after his patients had departed, reminded him that he had said he was eager to do what he could to help, and announced that what she needed was someone to talk to. When I was a kid, we used to play a game I thought rather silly. One person would be given, on a slip of paper, a ridiculous phrase, such as 'My father plays piano with his toes.' The point was to tell a story to your opponent, who, of course, had not seen the slip of paper, and to work your ridiculous sentence into it. Naturally, what you did was to tell a story full of outrageous statements, since your opponent had three challenges to discover which was the one on the slip of paper. Of course, the opponent almost never got it, because all the statements you made were as outrageous as 'My father plays piano with his toes.' This, in effect, was what Nicola had to do. I wanted to know Barrister's opinion of D. H. Lawrence, particularly of *The Rainbow*, and particularly of one incident in *The Rainbow*. Nicola had reread the appropriate section of the novel—fortunately, it came in the first seventy-five pages. She had to introduce this, however, along with lots of other literary discussion, so that it would not stand out from the surrounding material.

"Nicola did it beautifully.

"The second thing I 'did' was done by Nicola also. She fluttered, in her delightful way, around Barrister's office, and managed to discover, partly by asking him, but mostly by telling him—you miss a lot by not knowing Nicola's style—a bit of his routine.

"The third thing cost money. I sent Jerry out to a little town called Bangor, Michigan. He's on his way back now, but I spoke to him on the phone last night. Jerry had quite a time. He was looking for an old lady, but she was dead. Fortunately, it's a small town, and he managed to find the people the old lady had lived with before she died. They weren't related to her; she paid them for her room and meals, and for her care. This arrangement had been made

151

by Michael Barrister, who, of course, comes from Bangor Michigan.

"It was Michael Barrister who supported the old lady it was not a great amount of money he paid to the couple in whose house she lived, and as she grew older, and needed more care, he increased the amount. When she died, Michael Barrister made a quite suitable gift of money to the people who had cared for her over the years, and had given her, I suppose, the kind of affection that can't be bought.

"All this was straightforward enough, but I was after something else, and Jerry, with his boyish charm, managed to get it. He asked if the checks had ever stopped. After this build-up, you may perhaps not be overcome with astonishment to hear that they had. Barrister had sent a check every month, all through college, medical school, his internship and his residency. Then they stopped.

"The couple were decent people. They went on caring for her, but finally the financial burden became too great, and the man of the couple made a trip to Chicago. He managed to find that Barrister had gone to New York, and by going to the library and consulting a New York phone book, found his address. The man wrote to Barrister, and received back a letter of apology which explained that Barrister had been in financial difficulties, but was now all right. With the letter was enclosed a check for all the money due for the past months, and for the month to come. The monthly checks never stopped after that, until the old lady's death. But during those checkless months which had elapsed, the old lady had had a birthday, for which Michael Barrister had always sent her a letter and a present. The present was always the same: a small china dog, to add to her collection of china dogs. When the checks didn't come and the birthday was skipped, the old lady refused ever to hear Barrister's name again. She had called him Mickey, which no one else had done, but now she refused to refer to him, or to take anything from him again. The couple with whom she lived had to pretend to be supporting her, while taking Barrister's money, without which, of course, they couldn't get on. They didn't communicate with him any more, and the old lady never received another china dog."

"Touching story," Reed said. "Who was the old lady?"

"Sorry. I shouldn't have left that out. She had lived with Barrister's grandparents, and had cared for him when he was a boy. In the grandparents' will, all they had was left to their grandson, with a note added saying they were certain he would always care for the old lady. He always did.

"We return now to Nicola's conversation. She reported it to me word by word—in the event of all court stenographers being wiped out in a plague, together with all recording machines, I think Nicola would do nicely—but I will give you only the substance. Barrister has read *Lady Chatterley's Lover*. Otherwise, he has read nothing by D. H. Lawrence, whom he seemed, by the way, inclined to confuse with T. E. Lawrence, and gave it as his opinion, furthermore, that modern literature was off on the wrong track. It might be all very fine for professors and critics, but if a man read a book, what he wanted was a good story, not a lot of symbolism and slices of life.

"What Nicola discovered about Barrister's office had, I imagine, already been discovered by the police. He has a waiting room, several examining rooms and an office. Women, in varying stages of readiness, are treated in the examining rooms and talked to in the office. Barrister moves from one to the other, as does the nurse. If he is not in one, it is assumed he is in another. The ladies often have to wait quite a while, and are used to it—a fact, incidentally, which can be confirmed by anyone who has ever consulted a successful gynecologist. In other words, as you have already told me, Barrister did not have an alibi, though that good defense lawyer to whom you are always referring could make a great deal out of the fact that he was certainly having office hours at the time of the murder. Probably all the women who were there that day will have to be questioned closely, though not, thank God, by me.

"I now added to this information something Nicola had suggested the day after the murder, and something Jerry had discovered in an interlude with the nurse which I would, on the whole, rather ignore: that Barrister specialized in women unable to conceive, in women suffering from various 'female' problems, and in women wretched in their change of life. Incidentally, I called up my doctor, a conservative type on the staff of a teaching hospital, who was finally induced to tell me—all doctors, I've discovered, dislike the suggestion that medicine is ever badly practiced—that while many doctors treat women in menopause with weekly injections of hormones, he personally feels that too little is known about the effects of hormones and that they ought to be used only in cases of extreme need. Women, however, like the effects and are given hormones by many doctors. Do you want a drink?"

"Go on," Reed said.

"I'm now going to tell you a story, a story suggested to me by all these facts. Once upon a time there was a young doctor named Michael Barrister. He had passed his boards, and served his year of residency. He liked to camp and hike, particularly in what we seem to be calling the wilds of Canada, where you sleep out, or rent a room from a forester, or stay in an occasional hostel. Mike, if we call him that, went camping and met, in the wilds of Canada, a girl named Janet Harrison. They fell in love . . ."

"But her father was the mightiest man in the whole kingdom, and his but a poor woodsman."

"If you interrupt, Mommy isn't going to finish the story, and you'll have to go right to sleep. After a time the girl had to go home and so, pledging eternal love, they parted. Michael Barrister then met another man, a man who resembled him closely. They went off together on a hike. Mike spoke freely to the man, as one does with strangers; he told him a great deal about himself, but he did not tell him about the girl. One night the stranger killed Mike, and buried his body in the wilds of Canada."

"Kate, for the love of heaven . . ."

"Perhaps it was an accident. Perhaps it was only after Mike died in an accident that the stranger saw the situation he was in—perhaps he thought he would not be too readily believed—in any event, the idea came to him to take over Mike's identity.

"It was an enormous risk; a million things might have gone wrong, but none of them did. Or none of them seemed to. The bit about the old lady was a problem, but that seemed to resolve itself. The difficulty, of course, was that friends of Mike's would show up, but he could snub them—so that they would think that Mike had changed. It seemed as though the angels were on his side.

The body was never discovered. When he got letters, he answered them. The real Mike had a first-rate record, and the stranger had no difficulty setting up a practice. The malpractice suit was certainly a storm, but he weathered it.

"And then came the first huge problem: Janet Harrison. Her actual arrival was delayed many years. She had gone to nursing school, with the plan of joining Mike eventually in New York, and her letters spoke of this often. He wrote back trying, without harshness, to let the affair die down. He took longer and longer to answer her letters. When her mother died, she had to go home. But eventually, despite the delay, Janet Harrison, Nemesis, came to New York. She had never stopped loving him, and did not, or could not, believe that he had stopped loving her.

"He could not very well refuse to see her. He considered this, but she might talk, and it seemed better on the whole to know what she was up to. She soon discovered, of course, that he wasn't Mike. With a close-enough resemblance, it is remarkably easy, I imagine, to fool people. It does not occur to people that you are not who you say you are—simply that you have changed. But it is quite another matter to fool a woman who has loved a man and been to bed with him. She was a secretive type—that was a break for him—but she was determined to prove this Michael Barrister an impostor, and to avenge the murder of the man she had loved. She knew she was in danger—and she made a will, leaving her money to the man her Mike had admired, to the man who seemed like Mike. Unfortunately, if she collected any evidence, she didn't place it with the lawyer who made her will. She kept it in her room, or perhaps in a notebook she carried around with her. That is why he had to rob her room, even at tremendous risk, and go through her pocketbook after he killed her.

"She used to stand across the street and watch his office. She wanted to unnerve him, and undoubtedly she succeeded. But eventually she needed an excuse for the daily visits she wanted, and the presence of Emanuel gave it to her. Once, perhaps twice, she saw me emerge after a visit to Emanuel and Nicola. If she went to me, would I suggest Emanuel? She came to me, and I did. Had I not

155

suggested him—well, why should we worry about what might have happened?

"She took no one into her confidence, partly because she wasn't the confiding sort, any more than Mike was, partly because who would have believed her? Even though she is murdered, you are having trouble believing me now. One can imagine how the police would have treated a story like that.

"Dr. Michael Barrister knew he would have to act, certainly once she had started going to a psychoanalyst. On the couch she might say something, might even be believed. In any case, as long as she lived, she was a terrible threat. But he did not want to kill her. He was sure to be in the center of it; the closeness of his office to Emanuel's promised that. No matter where she was killed, the fact that she was in analysis would emerge, and he might be questioned. Perhaps, therefore, he could induce her to love him, could even marry her. He resembled remarkably the man she had loved. He knew women. He knew that they liked to be overpowered, and directed. He began to try to win her love. He must have thought for a time that he was succeeding. She allowed him to make love to her, yet something told him that she, too, was playing a game. She was trying to weaken his defenses.

"He knew the workings of Emanuel's home. Observation, talks with Nicola, glances through the court windows, told him all he needed. He had the rubber gloves of a surgeon. The telephone calls were child's play. He knew that Emanuel, given freedom, would gallop off to the park. If by some perverse chance Emanuel had not gone, Barrister was in no way committed; he could, at any moment, turn back. But Emanuel left, and Janet Harrison came to keep her appointment in an empty office. Barrister appeared. He probably told her some story of Emanuel's being called off, and led her to the couch, where, perhaps making love to her, he got her to lie down. Perhaps he pushed her back before he drove the knife home. No blood got on him, but if it had, he had only to climb in the court window of his office and wash himself. Of course, he took chances. He had to.

"But by killing her in Emanuel's office, he took as few as possible. He would have been involved no matter where she was killed; that is, his existence would have come to the attention of the police as a neighbor of her analyst's. He certainly could not kill her in his apartment—he never took her there. She lived in a woman's dormitory, a place in which people continually come and go. He killed her with Emanuel's knife on Emanuel's couch. This not only made Emanuel suspect, but rendered suspect anything Emanuel might say about what the girl had revealed in analysis. The girl had told him of me and Emanuel and Nicola—he knew we were friends, and he certainly picked up a lot of our past history from Nicola. Later, he sent the anonymous letter accusing me. Again he had a daring plan; he took enormous risks, and he won, or seemed to win. If he hadn't overlooked the picture, if Janet Harrison hadn't made the will, he would have got away with it."

"And if you, my dear Kate, hadn't obviously become a teacher because you were a novelist *manquée* . . . Talk about good stories! You ought to publish this one."

"You don't believe it."

"It isn't a matter of whether I believe it or not. Let's say I not only believe it; let's say it's true. You said the police might laugh at Janet Harrison. That's nothing to the way they'll howl at this. You haven't one shred of proof, Kate, not one—not even the whisper of one. The old lady? Mike was in financial difficulties, and his love affair put the old lady out of his mind. A novel by D. H. Lawrence? I can see myself explaining that to Homicide. An association in a dream related in the course of analysis to the chief suspect? The fact that the man he roomed with for one year didn't think the Mike he knew was likely to commit a murder? Murders are all too often committed by unlikely people—isn't it always the most unlikely person who turns out to have done it in books?"

"All right, Reed, I admit I haven't good evidence. But it's a true story, all the same, and it isn't just that I've become enamored of my invention. I knew you'd laugh. But don't you see that there must be proof somewhere? If the police with all their resources looked, they'd find it. Maybe somewhere there is still something with the real Mike's fingerprints—okay, so that's unlikely. Maybe Mike's body could be found. If the police really tried, they could find evidence. Reed, you've got to make them try. It would take Jerry and me years . . ."

"I should say so, digging up half of Canada."

"But if the police will only look, they'll find something. They might find who this man was, before he became Michael Barrister. Perhaps he was in jail somewhere. You could get his fingerprints . . ."

"Kate. All you've got is a fairy tale, beginning 'Once upon a time.' Find me evidence, one uncontrovertible piece of evidence that this man isn't Michael Barrister, and maybe we can get an investigation under way. We could hire private detectives, if necessary. All you've got now is a theory."

"What sort of evidence do you want? The real Mike wouldn't have forgotten that scene in *The Rainbow*. Am I supposed to find that the real Mike had a strawberry mark on his shoulder, like the long-lost sons from overseas in late Victorian novels? What would you accept as evidence? Tell me that. What?"

"Kate, dear, there can't be any evidence, don't you see? We can get Barrister's fingerprints, but I promise you they're not on record—he'd have known something as basic as that. Suppose we face Messenger with him—all Messenger can say is: He resembles Mike, but Mike has changed. Suppose you even discover that back in his medical school days Mike had a beautiful singing voice, that this Dr. Barrister is a monotone. Voices, I'm certain, can go. Though if you could discover that to be true, it would certainly be better than what you've got."

"I see," Kate said. "I've given you the motive and the means, but it's not enough."

"It's not, my dear. And I honor you too much to pretend respect for a theory that's a castle in the air. You've been worrying too much, and you're under strain. If I told the D.A. a story like this, I'd probably lose my job."

"In other words, Barrister has committed the perfect crime. Two perfect crimes."

"Kate, find some way I can help you. I want to. But life isn't fiction."

"You're wrong, Reed. Life isn't evidence."

"You admit you've made up this entire story. Kate, when I was in college, taking freshman English, the professor gave us a paragraph, and we were all to write a story

158

beginning with that paragraph. We were a class of twenty-five, and there were no two stories remotely alike. I'm sure, if you took a little time, you could make up another story, with Sparks or Horan as murderer. Why not try it, just to prove my point?"

"You forget, Reed, I've lots of evidence, though not the sort you find acceptable. The same sort of evidence proved to me that Barrister had known Janet Harrison. It so happens that Barrister got frightened and admitted it. But if he hadn't, I'd be sitting here now still trying unsuccessfully to convince you that those two had known each other."

"Perhaps you can face him with this story, and get him to admit it."

"Perhaps I will. An assistant D.A., I will tell him, knows about this tale, so why don't you kill me and prove to him that I was right?"

"Stop talking foolish. Where's that picture of the 'real Mike,' as we are now calling him? Get it, will you?"

Kate handed it to him. "One gets the feeling sometimes that it could speak. But I'd better not say that, I'll simply confirm you in your conviction that I'm round the bend. What did you want the picture for?"

"Ears. They don't show very well, do they? A good deal of work has been done to identify people by their ears. Too bad Real Mike didn't get his picture taken in profile. Then we could get a picture of Barrister's ear."

"Will you look into that, Reed? And please don't give me up as incurably demented. Perhaps I am just weaving fancies . . ."

"I know that conciliatory tone. It means you're about to do something I don't approve of. Listen, Kate, let's think about it. If we can come up with one piece of evidence that isn't literary, psychological or impressionistic, maybe we can interest the police. I'd rather go after a hormone dispenser, anyway, than a psychiatrist. Shall we go to a movie?"

"No. You may either go home, or you may drive me to the airport."

"Airport! Are *you* going to Bangor, Michigan?"

"Chicago. Now, don't start sputtering. I've been promising myself a visit to Chicago for a long time. They've got Picasso's 'Man with the Blue Guitar' there and I have

159

suddenly developed an uncontrollable desire to see it. While I'm gone you might read Wallace Stevens's poems inspired by the painting. He deals very effectively with the difference between reality and things-as-they-are. Excuse me while I pack a bag."

chapter 18

"COME into my office," Messenger said.

"Do you always work on Saturday?"

"If I can. I find it quieter than other days."

"And I have come to destroy the quiet."

"Only to postpone it. How can I help?"

Sitting across from Messenger, Kate confirmed for herself Jerry's impression. Messenger was lovable; there was no other word for this homely, gentle, intelligent man. "I'm going to tell you a story," Kate said. "I've told it once already; I'm becoming quite a storyteller. The first time it was received, if not with screams of hilarity, at least with grunts of disbelief. I'm not going to ask you to believe it. Just listen. Tonight you can tell your wife, 'I didn't get anything done this morning; some madwoman appeared and insisted on telling me some idiotic sort of fairy tale.' It'll make a nice anecdote for your wife."

"Go on," Messenger said.

Kate told him the story, just as she had told it to Reed. Messenger listened, smoking his pipe, disappearing at times behind a cloud of smoke. He emptied the pipe when she had finished.

"You know," he said, "when I went up to Mike in New York, he didn't at first know who I was. Natural enough, I guess; I'm not someone you'd expect to meet in New York. I noticed he'd got very elegant and didn't want to bother with me. There are those who are always ready to think they're being snubbed, and those who don't think anyone will ever snub them. I belong to the first class. Mike told me I'd changed. Well, I thought at the time, It's all in the eyes of the beholder; he's changed. But you know, I hadn't changed. There's one thing about having a face that could stop a clock—it doesn't seem to vary with the

161

years. But I wear glasses now, which I didn't used to do, so it seemed logical enough that it was that."

"You mean the whole story doesn't strike you as utterly fantastic?"

"Well, you know, it doesn't. The man I met in New York wasn't a beer drinker. I don't mean he told me that; we didn't have a drink, but he didn't look like a beer drinker. Mike didn't like hard liquor, just beer and wine with meals. Still, tastes change. I'm afraid your Reed Amhearst would say we ought to go into business together as writers of science fiction. Maybe we should."

"It's a deal. You do the science, I'll do the fiction. Reed would say I'm magnificently qualified. What I want now, Mr. Collaborator, is one fact. Like a strawberry mark on Mike's shoulder. Mike wasn't nearsighted, was he, or deaf in one ear?"

"I know what you want. I knew at that moment in your fairy tale when Mike met the stranger. But Mike wasn't nearsighted, or deaf, or a monotone, or an opera singer. The only thing I can think of is that Mike could wiggle his ears, you know, without moving any other part of his head. But that wouldn't do as evidence either. Besides, I'm told anyone can learn to do it, if he practices long enough. I have a lovely picture of your Dr. Barrister sitting at home, night after night, learning to wiggle his ears. You see, I'm rambling on, not being any use at all."

"I told you a crazy story, yet you didn't ring for the authorities and say, 'Get this woman out of here.' Believe me, that matters more than you know. Mike must have liked you enormously. Janet Harrison knew it; that's why she left you her money. You know, there's a nice crass motive I can hold out. If we can prove this tale, or get the police to prove it for us, you've got a much better claim to that money she left you."

"Unfortunately, that will make my testimony all the more suspect. The trouble, you see, is that I knew Mike only a year, and we weren't exactly Damon and Pythias. I don't remember when he told me that bit about the Lawrence novel—probably I asked him about his family because he never mentioned having any. For the most part, he didn't talk about himself. We discussed medicine, the advantages of different specialties—that sort of thing. Wait a minute, what about teeth?"

"I thought of teeth. I'm a reader of detective stories. The dentist in Bangor who looked after Mike's teeth died long ago; Jerry couldn't find any trace of his records. Probably the dentist who took over the practice from Mike's dentist kept only the records that were active, and even *he's* gone. It happens that I changed dentists about five years ago when the family dentist retired, and I called the dentist I go to now—you have no idea what a nuisance I've been making of myself—only to discover that all he has is the record of the work *he's* done on my teeth. The dentist who retired sold his practice, but the dentist who bought it hasn't kept records going back to the year one. The only dental record of me is of the work that's been done in the past five years, and that isn't much. Most of my fillings date back to my adolescence. You don't happen to know, for instance, that Mike had all his wisdom teeth extracted. If we could prove that, and this Dr. Barrister turns out to have four very present wisdom teeth . . ."

Messenger shook his head. "At the time, of course, I wasn't looking for anything. Being a resident is a very wearying and demanding business; often we weren't home at the same time. I don't even remember if Mike snored; I don't know if I ever knew. As a matter of fact, I haven't got a very good memory for personal things. My wife complains about this from time to time. I'm always complimenting her on hats she's had three years. I remember looking at my wife one day, and thinking, You're gray. But I hadn't noticed it happening. I'm sorry. You've come all this way and . . ."

"I could have telephoned. I wanted to come. There's a plane back this afternoon. I'll even have time to go to the museum."

"Why not come home to lunch with me? I'd like you to meet Anne. She's the most sensible, down-to-earth human being in the world. Maybe she'll think of something."

Kate was glad to accept the invitation. They were a nice family. After lunch, Kate and the two Messengers sat in the backyard, as the Messengers called it, and Kate told her story once again. Anne was not, like Kate and Messenger, a dreamer. Her reaction was more like Reed's. Yet as Kate was leaving, Anne said: "I'll be honest, Kate; I think this story was just logical enough for you to believe it at first, and since nothing you knew absolutely contradicted it, you allowed yourself to become convinced. I don't believe your story really happened. But it's not impossible that it happened, and if Dan knows something that can prove it, we've got to dig that something out. I'm more systematic than he is about everything except genes. I'll try to help him remember, in a systematic way. But please don't hope too much."

And Kate went to see the "Man with the Blue Guitar."

She was home by ten o'clock. The trip from Kennedy Airport had taken almost as long as the flight from Chicago, longer if she counted her wait for luggage, but even so, she was glad she'd gone. Reed called at ten-thirty.

"I know I met you at a political club," he said, "but I didn't know you were planning to emulate a political candidate. Do you think you might stay put now, say, for twenty-four hours? Did you get anything? Well, hope springs eternal. I, though I have not been winging through the wild blue yonder, have not been idle. I have consulted Ear Expert. Ear Expert said picture we have insufficient. Still, he'll try. We have set a detective, posing as a street photographer, to get a picture of the ears of Dr. Michael Barrister. It also occurred to me that there was probably a picture of your Mike in his college yearbook—possibly with ears. Or there may be a picture of Mike among the old lady's belongings, if we can find them. Ears don't change, I was fascinated to hear. Even a boyhood picture might do. Not that it's evidence, of course. The other side gets its own ear expert, who says 'inconclusive.' That's the trouble with expert evidence—you can usually get plenty for both sides. But I'm trying. What was Messenger like?"

"I wish I'd met him years ago and persuaded him to marry me."

"Oh, Lord, you *are* in a bad way. Shall I come and cheer you up? I can tell you about my lovely time with the grand jury. They decided the books we had gone to such great trouble to capture weren't pornographic. I don't know what the world's coming to, as my mother used to say."

"Thanks, Reed. I'm taking a grain and a half of Seconal and going to bed. Sorry about the trial."

164

"Never mind. I'm thinking of giving up law and writing pornography."

The ringing phone seemed to pull Kate up from depths far, far down in the ocean of oblivion. Frantically she fought her way to the surface. It was midnight.

"Yes," she said.

"Dan Messenger. I've woken you. But I thought you'd want me to. We've got it. You can thank Anne. Are you there?"

"I'm here."

"Anne told you she was systematic. She made lists, categories; we kept going over them. She started, in her logical way, with scars, though of course our present Barrister would have seen them too. I mean, if Mike had had his appendix out, this guy would go and get his appendix out. Always supposing he wanted to be that thorough. No bells went off when she mentioned scars, I'm ashamed to say, so we went on to other categories. Allergies, habits, times we'd gone out together. Are you still there?"

"God, yes!"

"Then she hit on one that seemed ridiculous; the category of clothes. One could hardly say this guy wasn't Mike because he didn't still have the old tweed jacket Mike cherished. Not that Mike did. I mean, I don't remember any tweed jacket. I said I didn't remember his clothes at all. We wore white almost all the time, including shoes. And then, you know, it came to me. Shoes. White shoes. I had only one pair—there wasn't any money in those days, and I'd got huge holes in the sole. It was raining, and the hole in the shoe worked like a pump. My feet were soaked, and so were my only pair of white shoes, and I asked Mike, who was off duty, if I could borrow his. Our feet looked about the same size, and even if Mike's didn't fit too well, at least they were dry. He told me I could borrow them, but that I'd find them a little hard to walk with. I asked him why. 'Because I wear a lift on one heel," he said; 'you probably haven't noticed it, most people don't. It's only five-eighths of an inch, but to a man with legs the same length, it will feel as though you're walking with one foot on the curb.' Well, I tried them on—they were too small, in addition, and I didn't

165

wear them. Still there? Grunt once in a while, will you? It's disconcerting with no sound at the other end, like talking into a stage phone. That's better.

"I haven't had much to do with orthopedics since medical school, but I think if a man once wore a lift, he would go on wearing it. Still, you'll have to check that. The great point is, Mike did have a scar, though I never saw it. But if he had an operation we can find a record of it; there's no problem about that. You're going to have to check on all of this, though, with an orthopedist, and the police.

"Mike didn't tell me about his scar at that time. I might have remembered it more readily if he had. Some months later Mike went back to the hospital when I knew he was off duty, and naturally I asked why. We didn't hang around if we didn't have to. He told me he wanted to watch a spinal fusion. He couldn't stay the whole time; it's a very long operation, sometimes eight hours. I think as an operation it's so recent, comparatively speaking, because they didn't have the proper anesthetic until recently. I asked him about the operation when he came back, and he said it wasn't as neat a job as his. 'My scar's like a pencil line,' he said. He told me he'd had a slipped disk, and they'd done the spinal fusion. The operation was successful enough, but when it was over he still had this terrible lower back pain. It was an old general practitioner in Bangor, he said, who cured it. I don't mean the operation hadn't been necessary—there was pressure on the nerve, the muscles in one leg were atrophying—but it was the old guy who cured the pain. He found out Mike's legs weren't the same length. There was seesaw motion in the pelvis. Mike had a lift put on his shoe, and that was it. So it's over to you, lady. I don't know how you're going to get your Dr. Michael Barrister undressed, but when you do, remember, the scar isn't that screamingly visible. I've found out this much for you: it runs up and down, over the lower vertebrae, for three to four inches. At some point, it loops out. That's where they fold the skin back. You might start by noticing if our friend wears a lift on his shoe.

"But remember this—even if your story is true, the murderer may have noticed. He may have tried on Mike's shoes. He may have looked the body over very carefully for scars, and found this one. If he wears a lift on one

166

shoe—and though I've racked my brain, I can't remember which—and if he's got a scar, your story may still be true, but we'll never, never prove it."

When Messenger, roundly thanked, had rung off, Kate called Emanuel. He was not, it turned out, asleep. Never a good sleeper, he was now an insomniac.

"Emanuel. This is Kate. I want you to call up an orthopedist. Well, all right then, the first thing in the morning. I want to know if a man who wears a lift on his shoe because his legs are of uneven length would ever decide to do without the lift. And I want to know if the scar from a spinal fusion could ever disappear. No, I don't want your opinion. I know you're a doctor. Ask an orthopedist. And he better be sure enough to swear in court. Sleep well."

chapter 19

SUNDAY night, or, more accurately, Monday morning at two A.M., there was a gathering at Kate's house—whether it was a celebration or a wake depended upon a guest who was not yet there. Emanuel, Nicola, Jerry and Kate were waiting for Reed. Kate had flirted momentarily with the thought of inviting Sparks and Horan, but Emanuel's unwillingness to meet his patients socially argued against the idea, even if it had had anything else to recommend it.

Reed had worked like a yeoman since early Sunday morning. Emanuel had apparently aroused his orthopedist from sleep, and instead of asking him questions, had simply persuaded him to call Kate himself. Kate had in turn reported the conversation to Reed. "You know how doctors are," she had said. "This one was just a shade this side of irritable, but I gather that for Emanuel's sake he didn't like to refuse to talk to me altogether. He probably thought I was writing a novel, and he answered my questions in the most long-winded, technical way possible. But then doctors are always indulging in either incoherence or oversimplification—if you want my opinion, I don't think they even understand each other. However, I did manage to gather one or two things."

"I don't suppose," Reed had answered, "you would care to tell me why you were interrogating an innocent orthopedist at such an ungodly hour Sunday morning?"

"I will tell you in time, and there is no such thing as an innocent orthopedist. They are all as rich as Rockefeller and as arrogant as swans. I know at least two, and am therefore able intelligently to generalize. Anyway, his information, much diluted, is this: Once someone has had a spinal fusion, he is marked for life as a man who has had a spinal fusion. That may sound a little obvious, but it was important to establish it. It's a long operation—which I knew already—and sometimes involves two surgeons, one who works on the spine and disc, and one who works on the nerves. It is unlikely in the extreme that anyone who had been cured of a back pain by the use of a shoe lift would ever abandon its use. I know that's not a *sequitur*, at least not yet, but just listen. What is a spinal fusion? Sorry, I forgot you laymen have such difficulty following a medical man. People get herniated, or get slipped discs—yes, I know they're getting them all the time, even dachshunds get them. In other words, a piece of cartilage between two vertebrae slips out of place so that it is pressing on the nerves in the spinal column. In severe cases, there will be a numbness in one leg. The commonest way of dealing with a disc which continues thusly to slip is to remove it, and fuse the surrounding vertebrae together. The fusion is done by taking bone from another part of the body—nobody else's bone will do, except an identical twin's—grinding it up (all right, I'm almost finished; no, I did not call you up on Sunday morning solely to deliver a disgusting medical lecture), and placing it between the vertebrae to be fused. The vertebrae thus eventually grow together into one solid piece, and the patient is left with a scar over the fused vertebrae. Are you with me?

"Here, my long-suffering Reed, is the point. Mike Barrister—my Mike, you know, not the one now in the office across from Emanuel—had a spinal fusion; also, he wore a lift on one of his shoes because his legs were of unequal length. No, of course he wasn't a freak. It's immensely common. But unless there is an extreme difference in leg lengths (that's rather hard to say) the person usually will compensate for it by an odd sort of rolling walk. However, once there is an injury to the back, the constant movement of the pelvis, because of the uneven length of the legs, causes acute discomfort."

"Kate," Reed had said, "are you trying to tell me, in your own way, which I must say has become exceedingly long-winded and full of unnecessary details, that Janet Harrison's Mike had an operation? When?"

"That, my pet, is what you, please, are going to find out. He probably had it in Detroit, which is, isn't it? the big-

169

gest city in Michigan; but that's just a guess. The lift on the shoe you will have to take Messenger's word for. Of course, if you're going to continue to be stubborn, I can call hospitals myself . . ."

"All right, I'll call the hospitals. Then what?"

"Then, my boy, we've got to get Dr. Michael Barrister undressed. I would hate to tell you some of the schemes that have been rushing through my fevered brain. I don't suppose you could get a search warrant."

"A search warrant is to examine premises, not persons, and I'll let you in on a horrible secret. You'd be surprised how few search warrants are ever issued. The head of the narcotics division testified the other day in court, and he admitted quite calmly that in thirty years his men had never obtained a search warrant. Citizens are, unhappily, but fortunately for the police, remarkably unaware of their rights. The police have a number of tricks for getting where they want, of which plain bullying is the chief."

"If I could only get in there when he was taking a shower."

"Kate, I'm not even going to listen to you for one more minute unless you promise, your solemn word-of-honor-hope-to-die, that you will not attempt to undress Barrister, see him undressed, lead him into any situation where he is likely to get undressed, or in any way involve . . ."

"Will you help, if I promise?"

"I won't even continue this conversation until you promise. I want your word. All right. Now let me call hospitals. They will tell me none of their clerks works on Sundays. No one works on Sundays, except you and your friends. I will then threaten and cajole. But we may have to wait, even so. I don't know to what degree the New York Police Department is willing to flex its muscles. Now, stop evolving schemes. I'll call if and when I get any news. And remember your promise."

Kate had had to wait until the afternoon, when Reed called again. "Well," he had said then, "I will not tell you what I have been through. I'll save the details till we are old and gray, and our brains have room only for memories. We have established the operation. Now, if I follow you correctly, you want to discover if Emanuel's neighbor, Dr. Michael Barrister, has had an operation for a spinal fusion and if he wears a lift on the heel of one of his shoes."

"You follow me perfectly."

"Good. Now here's a bargain; take it or leave it. I understand your feeling for Emanuel, the importance of this case to psychiatry's popular reputation, etcetera, etcetera, but I still don't like what this case is doing to you. You are giving up your work in the library, cutting classes, spending money like a drunken sailor, taking sleeping pills, flying all over the United States in a most abandoned manner, getting long-winded and leading young men astray. All this has got to stop. Therefore my bargain. I will tonight discover for you, provided Dr. Michael Barrister spends tonight at home, whether or not he has the scar from an operation, whether or not there is a lift on all his right shoes, or all his left shoes. If there is no scar, and no lift, I think the police will be very interested. We have, after all, established the operation. In other words, I'll admit this is your piece of evidence, and we'll look at Barrister much more closely, as a man with opportunity, means and motive. But, here's your side of the bargain. If Dr. Michael Barrister *has* a scar over any of his lower vertebrae, whether or not he has lifts on his shoes—for we haven't got any decent evidence that your Mike had lifts on his shoes (don't argue with me, I haven't finished)—if Dr. Michael Barrister has such a scar, then you agree to ignore this case, stop hiring Jerry, go back to your work. In short, you promise generally to return to your wonted ways. Is it a bargain? Never mind how I intend to undress Barrister; we'll discuss that after I've done it. Is it a bargain?"

And Kate had promised that it was.

Inviting Jerry and the Bauers to wait for Reed had been her own idea. They had discussed the case from every angle, up to and including what Kate now called her venture into "once upon a time." She told them of her bargain. She told them Reed would be late. And as the night wore on, she fed them coffee, which they drank, and sandwiches, which they did not eat. After a while, they could think of nothing more to say, and they fell silent. So silent that they heard the elevator and Reed's steps. Kate was at the door almost before Reed's hand was off the bell.

For the first time Reed met Emanuel, Nicola and Jerry. He shook the hand of each, and asked for a cup of coffee.

"I take it," he said, "that you all know what I was up to tonight. There are many ways the police use to break into an apartment. For example, they disconnect the lights in a house. The tenants rush out into the hall to see what the trouble is, and the police slip in through the open door. Once the police are inside, very few people will forcibly evict them. That scheme occurred to me, but I abandoned it for various reasons: Barrister lives in a new and elegant house on First Avenue; throwing the switch there would not be easy; more important, we wanted him undressed. That meant waiting until he had gone to bed, in which state he was unlikely to notice that the lights were out. We might simply have woken him and said we were inspecting a gas leak, but in that case it might be difficult to get him out of his bathrobe and pajamas. Therefore, I hit on the scheme of waiting till he had gone to bed, ringing the bell until he opened the door, and then demanding that he accompany us to headquarters for questioning. It was undoubtedly an odd hour to question someone, and we were prepared for indignation, but, of course, nothing ventured, nothing gained. So, a little after midnight, we went to call on Dr. Michael Barrister."

"Who is 'we'?" Jerry asked.

"'We' is your humble servant and a uniformed policeman. Uniforms are very useful for convincing people that one is, in fact, the police. Also, they generate a certain atmosphere of emergency which I was eager to have generated. The policeman who came with me did so as a favor. If I succeeded in my errand, as I told him, he would come in for a good deal of commendation; he might even be promoted. If I failed, I promised to see that none of the onus rested on him. I wanted him there, atmosphere apart, to have a witness as yet unconnected with this case. I was afraid that my connection with certain aspects of it"—he glanced at Kate—"should I be called upon to testify, might, in certain hands, be capable of misinterpretation.

"We succeeded in rousing Dr. Barrister from bed. He was, as I feared, wearing pajamas. He had, in addition,

172

thrown on a bathrobe. Had he slept in the nude, and opened the door that way, we would simply have engaged him in conversation, one in front, one in back. As it was, we had to ask him to dress and come down with us to 'Headquarters.' There is, actually, no such place as 'Headquarters,' but I wanted to be both as ominous and as vague as possible. After much shouting and threatening, and references to important men who were, I gather, the husbands of his patients, he consented to get dressed. He said he wanted to call a lawyer, and I told him he would be allowed one call from 'Headquarters,' according to regulations, may the blessed saints forgive me! Finally, he agreed to get dressed, but protested anew when the policeman followed him into the bedroom. I explained that this, too, was regulations, to be certain that he did not telephone or injure himself, or conceal a weapon, or hide anything. He flung into the bedroom, purple with rage, closely followed by the policeman, who had been carefully instructed by me. I had originally thought of telling the policeman to examine Barrister's shoes, but I abandoned the idea. We were going to succeed or fail in this outrageous enterprise depending on the scar, and it seemed as well to concentrate on that.

"The policeman followed his instructions well. Barrister flung off his bathrobe and pajamas, and as he bent over slightly to pull on his underpants, the policeman stepped up for a good look. His instructions, had he any doubt of what he saw, were to trip, falling on Barrister, to examine Barrister's back more closely, and then apologize. This might have been necessary had Barrister turned out to be an exceedingly hairy man; when skin is covered with hair, it is difficult to determine if it is scarred or not. But Barrister wasn't hairy.

"Needless to say, I waited for Barrister and the policeman as I suppose expectant fathers wait for doctors. The two of them came out of the room together, and the three of us went downtown. Eventually we aroused the D.A., who said it was time someone dug up some blasphemous evidence in this unprintable case."

Kate and Emanuel had risen to their feet. Nicola simply stared. It was Jerry who spoke.

"There wasn't any scar," he said.

"What have I been telling you?" Reed said. "No scar. He was examined again downtown. No sign of any spinal fusion. But the policeman put it best. 'Neatest bit of back I ever saw in my life.' he said. 'Not a mark on it.'"

epilogue

Six weeks later Kate sailed for Europe. There was no one to see her off, at her own request. She disliked *bon voyage* parties, preferring rather to lean on the deck rail waiting for Manhattan to slip away. She had a cabin to herself, second class, ample work to do, and the prospect of a pleasant and productive summer.

The evening newspapers, six weeks before, given the story by Reed (who liked to keep reporters on his side), had blazoned forth the headlines: "New Suspect in Case of Girl on Couch." The *Times*, picking up the news late, had put it more decorously. Emanuel and his patients settled back to the analysis of unconscious motives. The Psychiatric Institute made no comment—it never did—but Kate felt certain she could hear its collective sigh of relief echoing in the night.

Jerry had returned to driving a truck, and to Sally, who was becoming somewhat restive with the lack of attention. He had refused a bonus. Kate had pointed out that it was part of their original agreement, verbal but no less binding for that, but Jerry, adamant, had taken only his salary. Kate put the amount of the bonus in a bank, intending to allow it to collect interest until it should be withdrawn as a wedding present.

As the ship came abreast of Brooklyn, a view which Kate found productive of nothing but thoughts concerning human decadence, she went below. She walked through one of the lounges and was astonished to discover Reed, sitting in a chair, looking as though he had grown there. She stared at him.

"I," Reed said, "am going to Europe."

"Well," Kate said, "I'm relieved to hear you know it. I

thought perhaps you imagined yourself in the lobby of the Plaza. Are you on vacation?"

"Vacation and leave. I decided to come at the last minute, and have to share a cabin with two young men who make up in vigor what they lack in virtue, but at least I am here. Protection."

"Who are you protecting?"

"Whom. For an English teacher, you do have more trouble with your pronouns. I wanted to protect you, so to speak, in the quarantine period, to be sure the fever was gone."

"What fever?"

"Detective fever. I've known a few people with cases like yours. They invariably sail for Europe and trip over a body on their way to the shower. It was simply no good expecting myself to sit in New York, imagining you following clues and dropping literary allusions."

Kate fell into the chair beside him. Reed smiled, and then raised his arm to beckon a passing steward.

"Two brandies, please."